MINDWARP

TARA NINA

MINDWARP

Tara Nina

To obtain permission to excerpt portions of the text, please contact the author at
http://taranina.com

T.N.Books

New Jersey
2018

Published in the USA

Dedication

This work of fiction is dedicated to the
fine men and woman who diligently strive to
maintain this country's security. The Office of
Terrorism and Financial Intelligence (TFI) is a
branch of the United State's Treasury
Department. It is their job to protect our
financial system from outside threat.

Chapter One

Lightheadedness.

The sensation captivated every ounce of her brain when she woke on the chaise lounger. At the sight of an unfamiliar male hovering over her, Amelia gasped and scrambled upright. Wrong move. Her head spun, and a wave of nausea cramped her stomach. His heavily accented tone reached into her whirlpool of confused thoughts, calming and relaxing her within seconds. Her pulse slowed and her breathing shifted from erratic to normal as recognition returned. Doctor Riyad's office; she sighed as the memory surfaced.

Potted plants, a shaded window, a wooden Old World crafted desk, and a high-back leather chair came into view as her gaze darted around the room. In the corner stood a large privacy screen made of teak and etched with delicate flowers, vines, and birds. Plush carpet, pale blue walls, and soft lighting, along with ocean sounds piped in through hidden speakers, provided a peaceful setting meant to soothe skeptical patients. Which Amelia had been before her first visit—a true non-believer. Today was session two in a series of four hypnotic treatments to help her with weight loss. The scale standing in the corner reminded her of the reason she was here.

"How do you feel, Amelia?" Doctor Riyad's thick Middle Eastern accent made her think his words through before replying. At times, she had difficulty understanding him and had to listen carefully.

"I'm fine." She shifted in the seat. "Just a little thirsty."

Doctor Riyad nodded to his assistant, Mina, who disappeared, then returned in seconds with a small cup of water from the cooler outside his office door.

Mina handed her the cup. "Here, drink this. It should help."

Cool coated her throat, relieving the strange, desert-dry sensation. Odd, that itchy, burning sting in the back of her throat happened when she woke last time as well. Was it her body's reaction to being hypnotized? Amelia set the cup on the side table, moistened her lips, and then focused on the doctor's face. With all her specialized training, she'd never thought she could be hypnotized, but somehow he'd managed to accomplish the feat.

"When I see you next time,"—Doctor Riyad jotted a few notes on his pad—"I expect you to weigh four pounds less for a total loss of nine pounds."

"Not sure how this works," Amelia replied, swinging her legs over the edge of the dark-brown, leather chaise lounger, "but it has so far. We'll see if it helps with the total twenty-five I want to lose." She stood.

"Oh, it will." Mina bobbed her head in affirmation.

"I can only hope." Amelia smiled as she offered her hand to the doctor. "See you next week."

After her first session she'd had her doubts, until the scale dropped one pound, then two in a week's time. She'd managed minute changes before, but never three pounds in a week. By the end of two weeks, she'd lost a total of five and made her second appointment with the doctor. Curiosity was the main reason she'd returned.

Was it coincidence or actual results of his techniques?

When he accepted her hand in a firm shake, she noted his well-manicured nails. His expensive, tailored silk suit and expensive leather shoes made her think he had a successful business. How else could he afford such fine things? So far, his techniques had worked.

Strange, at both visits she hadn't seen another client in the waiting room, not when she arrived nor when she left. Surely there had to be others. Maybe his schedule allowed plenty of time between patients to maintain their privacy. Lord knows, she wouldn't want anyone knowing she'd resorted to hypnosis for weight loss.

Meeting his steady, dark-eyed gaze, he gifted her with a bright, white smile. "Don't forget, four pounds."

"I won't."

Amelia nodded to the assistant as she walked from the exam room and into the reception area. Five pounds lost in a matter of two weeks might not seem like a lot, but it surpassed the two-week totals in her history of fad diets.

Bright sunlight made her squint as she stepped out of the doctor's office onto the sidewalk. What a glorious day. She sighed, pulled sunglasses from her purse, and slipped them on. What a glorious day indeed.

* * * *

"It doesn't make sense," Nolan O'Connell stated under his breath.

Four files lay spread open on his desk. The faces of each woman stared back at him. Nothing particular stood out about any of them with the exception of their crimes. Individually, they'd burglarized the banks in which they were employed. In each incident, the stolen money hadn't been found. None of the women deposited it in any traceable account, nor did they hide it anywhere in their homes or known locations associated with them.

The money had to be somewhere. Combined, these women stole over half a million dollars. Money like that didn't just disappear. Nolan lifted the photo of the most recent female involved. Her history gave no hint of criminal tendencies. He flipped through the other three photos. Neither did any of those women's histories. Nothing about these cases made sense. Common, everyday employees stealing without any memory of having committed the crimes.

Worst of all, they couldn't remember what happened to the money. Nolan sighed heavily as he placed the pictures back into the proper files. As lead Treasury Agent on the case, the responsibility of tracing the money trail had landed in his lap. There had to be an explanation. He relaxed into the high-backed, leather chair and stared out the window as he ran through the information he'd gathered.

In six months, four different women had embezzled large sums of money with no recollection of having done so. As if the memory of the events somehow magically disappeared from their brains. Nolan straightened. What if they'd been brainwashed into committing these acts?

Excitement coursed through him as possible scenarios fired at a rapid rate, piecing together a slim but semi-credible theory. Who would do such a thing to these women? Throughout TFI—the Treasury Bureau of Terrorism and Financial Intelligence—whispers of a possible new terrorist threat had circulated for months. The financial accounts of several known terrorist sympathizers were being monitored, but nothing actionable had surfaced. That didn't mean the research into the matter stopped. No, on the contrary, it increased the effort to prove the United States Treasury and financial markets were safe. Nolan took a deep breath. Had he stumbled onto the possible rumored new threat? If so, how had they managed such a feat? Who were they? Most important, where would they strike next?

Nolan gathered four colored tacks and walked to the wall map of Kentucky. If a terrorist sect was behind the thefts, why choose his state as their place of business? Why not New York City, the financial capital of the world? One by one, he located the venues and inserted tacks in the order the crimes occurred: white at Brandenburg, green at Shepardsville, blue at Elizabethtown, and red at Radcliff. Each location fell within a fifty mile radius of . . . No way! He snorted. No one had ever broken into that vault.

It didn't mean someone hadn't thought about it. He returned to his desk, sat in his chair, and simply stared at the colorful conglomeration of tacks on his map. As a TFI Treasury Agent, he had to evaluate every aspect of the United States' financial system. His training entailed reviewing detailed terrorism plots and dissecting them to follow the money stolen to finance crusades against America. He'd never failed an assignment and had no intention of starting now. The missing bank money had to be somewhere and he planned to locate it.

One particular vault amazed him during his internship as a trainee. Truth be told, that was the main reason he'd chosen the small, new Louisville office as his site. A smile upturned his lips as he sifted through the information in his head on the Fort Knox Bullion Depository. It would take more than one person to break into that place. *If,* it were even possible. He shook his head in an effort to dislodge the inconceivable notion.

Again, he opened the folder and lifted the four photos. What did these women have in common? Something had to link them together. He'd spent hours pouring over the information. Their statements seemed vague and confused. Had they been brainwashed? Had his initial thought been right? He couldn't stop revisiting that probability.

Over time it had become apparent that terrorist organizations desperate to get a toe-hold in America brainwashed and instilled ideas into innocent victims as part of their regimen. If they couldn't recruit new members, terrorists turned to alternative means to gather the hands they needed to accomplish their twisted missions. Over the years, several *sleepers* had been discovered and stopped before they completed the assignments. Could there be a terrorist cell in the area? What if they'd found a unique way to program people to steal for them?

Determined the involved women were pawns in a much larger game, Nolan decided to investigate his theory and the women more thoroughly. If the missing money had landed in the terrorists' hands, there was no telling what they were funding. A bomb, an attack on American soil . . . God, please not another 9/11. Well, it wasn't going to happen. Not if he could help it. He'd taken an oath when he joined this department to protect the financial system from national security threats. In his book, this landed under that oath.

Nolan gathered the files and stood. He needed to personally interview these women. Something must've been missed. Some question left unanswered. There had to be a common thread that bound them. If these women had been brainwashed, he wanted to know by whom and what they planned to hit next. He stopped in front of the Kentucky wall map, eyeing the tacks. Even though the theory was thin and lacked enough evidence, it refused to let loose of his instinct. He sighed. Man, he hoped he was wrong.

Nolan tucked the files in his large, messenger-style briefcase, then set it beside the coat rack. He slipped his gray jacket over his starched, white, button-down, long-sleeved shirt. After straightening his gray and white striped tie, he grabbed the only accessory that didn't fit the dull-suited, bureau criteria. After running a hand through his hair, he donned the Western Outback fedora. Nice. He smiled as he slid his thumb along the brim of his version of the cowboy hat. He loved the tan Akubra fur felt.

As he grabbed his briefcase, he made a mental note to call his parents before the weekend. If he didn't, they'd probably pop in for a visit and he didn't have time to play host to his retired folks. Not this weekend; not if he planned to compile evidence to either support or disprove his theory. He hoped for the latter. Terrorists were the one thing he hated more than money launderers for drug lords. He shut his office door, locked it, and headed for the elevator.

* * * *

"Hey, Amelia, I've been looking all over for you."

The sound of Terrence's voice grated on her nerves. Its nasal tenor and droll monotone practically induced sleep whenever he managed to corner her and force her to listen to his dry monologue about whatever subject he chose. Amelia rolled her eyes to the heavens and prayed the elevator doors closed before he reached them. Even though she repeatedly pressed the *door close* button, his foot slid between the stainless steel, preventing her escape. Unfazed, he lunged inside, waving a flyer in her face.

"Great, I caught you. You mustn't have heard me calling." He adjusted his black, plastic-frame glasses. "When I left the grocery store last night, I found this on my windshield and thought of you."

Though she didn't want to, she took the crumpled paper. One look and confusion bunched her brows. "What's this announcement about an eco-friendly, health-food deli grand opening got to do with me?"

Terrence reached around her and pressed the first floor button. The hair on his forearm brushed her elbow and she had to fight the urge to cringe from the unexpected touch. Since his arrival almost six months ago, his persistent pursuit had kept her on guard whenever he was around. She tried politely to maintain a distance from him. In the cramped elevator, he seemed oblivious to the sanctity of personal space.

"Well," he stated on a garlic-laden breath within a couple of inches from her face. "I understand you've made progress with your weight situation and thought we could go there and celebrate."

She crinkled her nose against the odor. If she had a mint, she'd give it to him. "My weight situation?" She stepped back, trying to capture a garlic-free breath. Oh my God, he didn't just imply something about her weight. Out of the corner of her eye, she caught the reflection of her backside in the stainless steel. The battle of the bulge had been a continuous struggle her entire adult life, but her problems weren't any business of his. Heat filtered up her spine, making her stand straighter. Chin tilted, she stared him directly in the eye as she shook the flyer at him. "Are you implying I'm fat and should try eating this stuff?"

"For my taste,"—he wagged his eyebrows—"no. I like my women with a bit of meat on their bones. I heard you'd dropped five, and to show that I support your effort, I'd like to take you to lunch. That flyer simply suggested a healthier choice."

"I'm not *your* woman." She kept her tone as calm as she could muster through the angry constriction in her throat. The extra twenty-five pounds she carried was none of his concern. Besides, her latest weight loss attempt seemed to be working. This morning, the scale verified another pound had disappeared. The hypnosis techniques had helped her with sugar cravings to the point she wasn't eating ice cream and candy bars everyday.

"Not from my lack of trying. You just seem to always be busy."

The fact she shot mental daggers at him somehow she doubted would faze him if he knew. He'd asked her out many times and she'd given him polite excuses, but he simply didn't seem to comprehend she wasn't interested.

"I have noticed you've dropped a little. So the hypnotist is working?"

The doors slid open and Amelia pushed past him into the lobby. As far as she was concerned, this conversation was over. Heat rolled off her as anger speared through her. How did he know about the hypnotist? That was supposed to be a secret between her and her best friend Louisa. His hand clamped around her elbow and nearly threw her off balance in mid-stride. Before falling, she righted herself, jerked her elbow from his grip, then whirled and faced him.

Her gaze darted around and she kept her

voice low. "How do you know about that?"

She certainly didn't want any of the higher-ups overhearing she'd been hypnotized. It might not set well with their ideals of what was and wasn't a security risk for her position at Fort Knox.

"I gave Louisa the hypnotist's business card a couple of months ago." Terrance didn't give her a chance to speak. Her jaw gapped open as he rambled on. "I got it from Hubert. You know, the new janitor for your floor, I ran into him at the one-hour dry cleaner on Rosemary Street. Started up a conversation with him, you know, welcome him to the neighborhood. Seems he's not so nice. Doesn't like being spoken to, said I talk too much, grabbed the card from the rack of local business cards on the wall and handed it to me. Said maybe it could help me learn to shut up. Can you believe that?" He shrugged with a laugh. "One look at the card and I thought you could use it. Instead Louisa tried it. How did you think she got over that nail-biting tendency of hers?"

Staring at him, Amelia couldn't believe he'd stated all that without so much as catching a breath. She closed her mouth, tightly. He had to be speaking utter nonsense. Louisa had told her she'd quit by keeping lemon juice on her nails and the taste turned her off. If what Terrence said was true—and she doubted it—Louisa had lied. She huffed as she faced Terrence.

"Terrence, I'm sorry it's come to this," she gasped out between clenched teeth. She couldn't wait to get hold of Louisa. Terrence had to have found out about her visits to the hypnotist through her. It didn't make sense why Louisa would say anything to him. They both knew Terrence was a bit on the talkative side. Even if he did give her the hypnotist information, Louisa was her friend and this was supposed to be a secret.

Taking a deep breath, Amelia reined in her

anger. Terrence wasn't at fault for Louisa's loose lips. She just wished this hadn't been shared with *talkative* Terrence. It wasn't his looks that turned her off. It was his non-stop chitchat. The black plastic frames, small dark eyes, and slicked back, short hairstyle gave him a "Buddy Holly" appeal. She'd dated the nerdy type before and enjoyed intellectual conversations.

His overall general appearance was that of a harmless individual, but his consistent chatter kept her on high alert in order to avoid being cornered by him. Even though he wasn't her preferred type, he'd been nothing but nice to her . . . persistent, but nice.

She kept her manner calm. "I don't think it's wise to date coworkers. That's why I think it'd be best if we just stay friends. Okay?"

Terrence straightened as he stared directly at her. She couldn't read him. His eyes held a dark mystery she had no desire to unravel. Something about him didn't sit well with her gut.

"I understand at the moment you hold no romantic interest in me. As a man, I find you a challenge, a quest of perfect beauty." When she opened her mouth to speak, he raised his hand to shush her. "For now, I'll accept the fact we're merely friends and coworkers. As your friend, I thought it might be nice if you knew of another facet to weight loss, since you seem to be on a perpetual diet. I gave that business card to Louisa to give to you, but she tried it first on her minor bad habit. I guess she had to see if it worked before giving it to you. From what I've noticed in the lunchroom, the diet foods you keep carting in for lunch don't seem appealing."

"They aren't," she begrudgingly admitted. He had her there. The majority of the pre-packaged diet foods lacked flavor. If she were honest, she lost the same five pounds repeatedly. Next visit to the hypnotist would be the chain breaker in this awkward cycle if she managed to reach her goal of four more pounds for a total of nine.

"Besides, there's something you should know." He lowered his voice as he guided her across the lobby and out the front door. "I happened upon a missive from the Secretary of the Treasury Department to Administration. Within the next two months, a new health advisory for all employees will be implemented. A part of it pertained to overweight personnel. They plan to *suggest* that any individual who doesn't meet military health requirements must attend a *Get Fit* boot camp."

Amelia had heard of such places springing up all over the country. The camps drilled healthy living criteria into unhealthy participants and helped them change their lifestyles for the better. When she'd first heard of it, she'd thought about trying it. But the cost outweighed her pocketbook and in her heart she didn't have what it took to survive the stringent boot camp regimen. Rolling out of bed in the wee morning hours, jogging for miles on end, exercising, and eating the basic rations didn't fit in her agenda of things to do with her life.

"Are you sure about this?" It didn't surprise her that a new health mandate targeting civilian personnel might be forthcoming. If they enforced this change, would she be out of a job for noncompliance? She'd have to check into it. In the meantime, she desperately needed to shed a few pounds to avoid the humiliation of fat camp.

"Working in the mailroom has its perks," Terrence proclaimed in a low tone. "Even though I like you the way you are, it might be in your best interest to continue using this hypnotist. It shows he's helping you with what you consider to be a problem. If I remember right, his ad claimed he could heal certain problems such as smoking, addiction, overeating, and sexual dysfunction."

"Seems he can do it all." Still skeptical, Amelia pictured the two-sided business card on her table at home by the phone.

Kalil Sayyid Riyad, Master Hypnotist
Follow the path to inner healing through Hypnotism.
Guaranteed to help you find the natural healing potential you possess
to correct the following:
Smoking Habits, Drug Addiction, Obesity, & Sexual Dysfunction
& any other minor bad habit.

Amelia snapped out of her thoughts at the sound of Terrence's voice. "I doubt you have any sexual dysfunctions. If you did, I'd be more than happy to help you rectify them through trial and error."

She couldn't believe he'd just said that as she tried to maintain a cool façade. Digging the keys from her purse, she turned down the aisle to her car, hoping he'd stop following her. There wasn't one feature about him she found attractive. Nothing set her heart to flutter or made her hunger to hear his voice. That's what she wanted . . . a man who'd make her quiver inside with a simple look. Glancing over her shoulder at Terrence, she knew he wasn't that guy. At work, she tolerated him and did her best to avoid him, especially since he continually asked her out. A sliver of her considered him harmless, but the rest of her entire being didn't trust him. Not that he'd ever given her a reason not to. Her instincts hummed something wasn't right with him. Never had she ever known someone who couldn't take a hint and didn't shut up.

Amelia rolled her eyes and grappled for an ounce of niceness. The inner voice of her conscience whispered, *He didn't have to share the information he'd found in that missive with you.* No, she shook her head, he didn't. He did it because he liked her, even though she didn't feel the same about him. At her car, she unlocked the door, opened it, and tossed her purse along with the deli flyer to the front passenger seat.

She kept the open car door between them. "Thank you, Terrence, for letting me in on this info about fat camp. I do appreciate it."

"My pleasure." His smile broadened and she thought she saw a diamond embedded in one of his teeth. Funny, she'd never noticed it before, but then again, she tried not to stand this close to him at any given time. "How about I buy you and Louisa lunch tomorrow? It won't be a date. Just lunch, you, me, and Louisa at the new deli. Give the health food a chance."

On the spot, Amelia met his dark gaze, but couldn't read his intent. Was he just being friendly or did he have something else in mind? She hoped for a swift exit on this one. "I'll ask Louisa and get back to you."

"I already did. She said she'd go as long as you did. So, I can count on you both for lunch?"

He didn't give her a chance to answer, but spun on his heels and marched two aisles over to his car. *Ambushed*. That's how she felt. Ambushed by Terrence. Telling her about the missive had been his way of giving himself an edge. First, he'd shared crucial information with her to soften her up. Second, he told her he was the one who gave Louisa the perfect solution to Amelia's weight problem—the hypnotist. Third, now she owed him. At least that's how she figured he saw it.

She slid into her car, grabbed her cell phone from her purse, and hit the speed dial button number two. It rang twice while she started her car.

Louisa answered. "Hello."

"Did you tell Terrence you'd go to lunch with him if I went?"

"Yeah, but I figured I was safe. You never say yes to him."

"Your plan failed." Amelia sighed heavily. "Looks like we're having lunch with him."

"How did that happen?" Amelia could almost see the surprised look on Louisa's face through the phone.

"Meet me at my place and I'll explain."

As soon as Amelia pressed the gas pedal and began backing out, she stomped on the brake nearly missing a small-sized man. She lowered her window. "Sorry. Didn't see you."

He smacked her trunk and cussed at her. "Crazy bitch!"

Mumbling something she couldn't understand, he shuffled away. Amelia collapsed into the drivers seat, regaining her composure when it hit her. That squirrely-looking, small-statured man was the janitor Terrence had mentioned. Hubert, she thought he'd said was the man's name. She looked around for him to apologize again, but he had disappeared somewhere between the other parked cars.

Taking greater care, she backed from her spot, drove slowly from the lot, wondering where the hell he'd come from. He hadn't been there when she started backing out. It was as if *poof* he magically appeared behind her car.

Chapter Two

Nolan tossed his briefcase and hat on the front passenger seat. He unbuttoned his suit jacket, and hung it on the back of his seat. For several moments, he stared at the barbed wire fence that ran around the entire Kentucky Correctional Institute for Women. Over the last five hours, he'd interviewed three of the four women involved in the bank thefts. The drive to KCIW in Peewee Valley equaled thirty minutes of his time. Interviewing the last inmate would have to be by phone. She was incarcerated at Gatesville Women's Prison in Texas and flying there didn't fit into the department's tight budget.

The answers he'd gained so far left him baffled. Nothing about the events remained clear in any of their memories. Each adamantly denied committing the crime—not uncommon for convicted criminals. He sighed. Were they lying to him? His gut instinct screamed *no*. Something didn't add up.

Nolan slid into his car, closed the door, and started the engine. What bothered him the most . . . clearly they were innocent pawns in some twisted plot. Similarities threaded their stories. Every question he asked, their answers were related by minute details, but different. Yet, they were located in different cell blocks with no chance of meeting. The opportunity to speak hadn't occurred. He'd double checked that point when he spoke with the guards and the warden.

Surely he'd missed something. Information from their files flipped through his head as he turned out of the parking lot. Not long on the highway, traffic stopped. Twenty cars ahead of him, a tractor-trailer had jackknifed and spilled its cargo, scattering cases of live chickens all over the roadway. Clean-up crews were on the scene, so he hoped it wouldn't take too much longer to rectify the mess and get traffic moving again. Nolan put his car in park, relaxed in his seat, and glanced at the others stuck around him.

The guy in the car next to him lit one cigarette off of the other as he steadily chatted on a cell phone. He noted in the rearview mirror a woman sat munching on a bag of snacks. Two women got out of the car in front of him, strolled to the trunk, and opened it to reveal an abundance of shopping bags. No doubt they'd spent their day at the mall. *Shopaholics*, he snorted. *Shopaholics.* His eyes widened as he sat erect, glancing at the individuals who surrounded his vehicle. The guy lit another cigarette and the woman behind him now had a different snack in her hand. What did a chain-smoker, a binge eater, and a pair of shopaholics have in common?

Addiction. The word hit him square between the eyes. Nolan unhooked his seatbelt, leaned over to the passenger seat, and opened his briefcase. The theory brewing made his adrenaline race. He grabbed the women's files and thumbed through each of their personal medical histories. He noted each corrected a malady without remembering the steps taken for the remedy. Two quit smoking, but couldn't remember how they'd done it. The third one's doctor made a note of unexplained rapid weight loss. After a dozen different tests, they determined no ailment caused the weight drop. The fourth woman's nervous facial twitch disappeared, but she didn't know why. She claimed it had simply stopped.

A horn blared, jarring Nolan from his thoughts. Lifting his gaze, he saw traffic had resumed. Tossing the files back into his briefcase, Nolan returned his attention to the road. These women's lives had been tipped upside down just like that truck's cargo. Nolan sighed, glancing at the mess. What if there was a reason behind these sudden changes in their lives? What measures had they taken to rectify their bad habits? It seemed odd to him that each made a life-altering change within the months prior to committing the crimes— yet had no recollection of how they'd done it.

There had to be a connection. Determination churned in his gut. At the first exit, he dropped onto a side road that brought him in the back way to the Louisville Treasury Department building. After six, most had left work for the day. He swung into an empty space at the rear of the building. The department he needed would be more easily accessed through that corridor. Nolan swiped his ID card and pressed his hand to the imprint recognition system.

The lock released and he entered. A night guard making rounds greeted him. After exchanging a few words with him, Nolan hurried on. Tonight he was on a quest— solving the puzzle of four incarcerated females and hopefully setting their lives right along with making sure the missing money hadn't been used to finance a terrorist sect.

* * * *

When Louisa left, Amelia closed and locked her door. She shuffled through the events of the night and focused on the most important points. Louisa had visited the hypnotist because Terrance had given her the card to give to Amelia. Instead, she'd kept it to use for herself, try it out first, and see if it worked before giving Amelia another false hope on the weight loss train. She sighed as she ran a bath. Questions about the hypnotist and his methods tumbled through her head as she sank into the tub. Closing her eyes, she recalled the conversation that disturbed her most.

When asked, Louisa remembered smelling something right before she went under, but she'd thought it was some sort of incense. The fact she woke thirsty and dizzy after being hypnotized added to Amelia's concern. The more she thought about it, the more these minor things fueled her growing anxiety. Like herself, Louisa had never seen any other clients at the doctor's office. This propelled Amelia's suspicions into overdrive.

It was Louisa's admission of having odd dreams since visiting Dr. Riyad that had Amelia's gut knotted and mind shifting through different scenarios. Were these dreams somehow related to being hypnotized? Were they implanted suggestions by Dr. Riyad? Or, were they simply dormant or forgotten memories resurfacing triggered by the sessions?

The more she thought about it, the less she understood. Vague images flashed inside her head as she struggled to remember. She even shared the sensation with Louisa of forgetting something. Neither could figure out what they'd forgotten but sensed it was important. Things didn't add up. Never having been hypnotized before, she couldn't be sure if the issues she and Louisa experienced were simply side effects. One thing she decided, she intended to find out.

There were a few things brewing in her brain she just couldn't stop thinking about. Had she spilled secrets of her job under hypnosis? Doubt sprang to life. Fear gripped her soul. Maybe this hadn't been the smartest choice. Amelia swallowed hard and attempted to get a grip on her overactive imagination. Could she lose her highly-classified position at Fort Knox if her boss found out about this?

Amelia sat upright in the tub. She loved her job as an accountant with the United States Bullion Depository. Her parents were proud to have their only daughter working for such a distinguished organization. Though she knew they'd keep her secret, she didn't tell them of her most recent promotion. She'd been selected as one of the four individuals needed to open the vault. With the way the locks were designed, it required more than one person to work the combination at the same time. Her gut clenched. Had she spilled her series of numbers to the hypnotist? Panic thrashed through her as she breathed deeply, trying to gather her thoughts.

The one thing that eased her conscious— out of the four of them, no one knew which set of numbers actually opened the vault. Standing, she grabbed a towel from the rack, stepped out of the tub, and dried off. Even if she had relinquished her combination under hypnosis, she knew he couldn't do anything with it. Four people simultaneously inserting their codes were necessary to open that vault. Besides, she sighed in relief, a thief would never make it through the security. Every muscle froze as an idea slammed into her.

What if Dr. Riyad implanted something into her brain? What if he knew where she worked and was using her to steal from Fort Knox? Amelia shook her head. That idea didn't make sense. No one had ever successfully stolen from Fort Knox and they weren't about to now. Not with her help. She ran the towel through her hair. It had to be the fact she was tired that her thoughts twisted into such an impossible scenario. With her eyes closed, dark images flashed inside her lids but no matter how hard she concentrated, she couldn't distinguish what or who she saw. They were too vague and distorted. Mumbled words echoed inside her head, causing her to shiver.

She hung the damp towel on the back of the bathroom door, walked into her bedroom, and dressed in her favorite pajamas. The yellow cotton pair with parrots imprinted all over them gave her a sense of comfort as she slid under the covers. Her brain ached from system overload when thinking of Dr. Riyad. One thing she decided for sure as she turned off the bedside lamp . . . Tomorrow, she'd research hypnotism Web sites and learn more about the process. If she were lucky, maybe she'd find documentation of patients who'd experienced similar sensations of forgetfulness, woke up thirsty after a session, and suffered strange dreams. There had to be others out there who felt some sort of odd occurrences due to hypnosis.

At least that's what she hoped and that her idea of Dr. Riyad planting some sort of subliminal command was completely absurd.

Chapter Three

"Everything is going as planned?"

"Yes, the main individual needed for this job shall be finished with her programming after two more sessions." The heavily accented voice of Dr. Riyad paused then sounded concerned. "I don't like leaving Louisa's memory intact of her visits here. It opens the way for error. We shouldn't have included her in this project."

"They are best friends. It must be this way or else it would raise too much suspicion between them."

"Still—"

"My friend," he cut in, "you worry too much. I shall be there to whisper the command in her ear that will rid her mind of any memory of you or your work."

"You'd better be right. *He* will not accept failure."

"In this, we shall not fail." He hung up the phone. The subtle threat didn't go unnoticed. But it wasn't the first time in his line of work he'd been threatened and it probably wouldn't be his last.

It should bother him that his accomplice, Riyad, didn't seem to trust him, but it didn't. Was it because they weren't of the same nationality? Ah, he sighed to himself. Racism breeds well among religious fanatics. For years, he'd played one sect against another and worked for the highest bidder to regain whatever artifact they claimed belonged to them. As a renowned thief, it didn't matter who the item truly originated with; what mattered was the payment he received for stealing it.

According to his latest employer, he'd been recruited for a higher purpose. The goal thrilled him to the core of his black heart. Retrieve the Sacred Diamond of Shabib. Every ounce of research he'd done led him to one location. Rumored to have been stolen hundreds of years prior from some long forgotten sheik, it had been locked and sealed behind one of the world's most famous vaults.

A vault from which nothing had ever been stolen—Fort Knox.

The thought of it made his mouth water. He smiled, kicked off his shoes, and dropped into the raggedy recliner in front of the television. He'd not have to stay in this rented dump much longer. If all went as planned, that diamond would be in his hands within the next three weeks. Once his cut of the cash was deposited in his Swiss bank account, he'd be in Acapulco, basking in the sun and picking up some sweet honey to help him spend it.

Ah, if Amelia only knew the truth about him. For this job, he'd chosen an inconspicuous, common look to blend in and get the only position available at Fort Knox when he'd applied. Not his normal high profile, rich-playboy gig, but for the money, he'd act the part. Gain access to any of the four people in charge of the combination and lead them to Dr. Riyad for programming.

He kicked back in his chair as images of Amelia filled his thoughts. Maybe she'd date him if she discovered his superb financial status and saw him without the disguise. Nah, he shook his head. She didn't seem the type to be enticed by money, nor would she hang with a thief. She appeared to be too much of a tight-laced do-gooder to him. He laughed as he picked up the stack of take-out menus on the table beside the chair.

"Don't get emotionally involved." After reprimanding himself, he flipped through the menus. Women came and went in his life. Money always lured the hot, tight-bodied bimbos. *But just once . . .* He sighed as he settled on Chinese food.

"Ah, it'd be nice to sample a full-bodied babe like Amelia." He huffed as he dialed to order another night's one-person meal.

* * * *

Dead tired, Nolan made the final trek up a flight of stairs to his second story apartment. The usual greeting met him when he opened the door.

"Hello, Nolan."

"Hello, Pete." He shut the door, locked it, then walked to the coffee table and set down the box.

"Time for *Jeopardy*?"

"Of course, Pete." He picked up the remote, turned on the TV, then pressed the button that would play the show he recorded daily for Pete.

It didn't matter what time of day Nolan returned home, it was time for *Jeopardy* in Pete's mind. The moment the familiar game show music started, Pete bobbed and mimicked the tune. Nolan couldn't believe his parents had turned Pete into a *Jeopardy* addict. Twelve weeks in their care, while he attended specialized training courses for the bureau, had turned his pet African Gray Parrot into a game show contestant junkie.

"Awck, I'll take Shakespeare for a thousand, Alex."

Nolan couldn't help but smile at Pete's perfect enunciation. If nothing else, he'd have to give his folks credit for extending Pete's vocabulary. Pete's round of answers and questions continued as Nolan entered the bathroom. With the long day behind him, he headed for the shower.

What he'd found earlier astounded him. How had it been missed? *Because the women committed the crimes separately and not as a gang,* he reminded himself. The evidence in each case alone convicted them individually. With the money still missing, he'd been given all four cases to study. Wanting to clear his head, he closed his eyes and freed his mind of all thought. The hot water soothed his tired system and rinsed the ache from his flesh.

Fifteen minutes later, Nolan stepped out of

the shower, clean, relaxed, and refreshed. After slipping on a tee shirt and sweats, he fed Pete who uttered a polite, "Thank you," then resumed playing the game. From the freezer, Nolan retrieved the single serve dish he'd brought home from last Sunday's dinner at his parents' house. A few minutes in the microwave and the essence of corned beef and potatoes filled the air. His stomach rumbled as he threw together a simple salad and poured a glass of wine.

While eating, he reviewed his notes from the conversations with the convicted bank thieves. More than ever, his gut told him these women were innocent pawns. Local law enforcement for each town investigated the crimes until the feds took over. Since no obvious link between them had been found, they weren't considered a gang. Each woman had been caught within twenty-four hours, and the gap of time between each incident added to that train of thought. Now that the feds were out of it and the women were in jail, the case became the Treasury Department's problem to track the money.

Nolan washed the dishes and set them in the drain. He refilled his wineglass, grabbed the one thing he'd not returned to the evidence vault, relaxed in his recliner, and thought through the information he'd discovered earlier. A visit to the evidence vault gained him access to four large, padded manila envelopes containing miscellaneous items that belonged to the convicted women. One by one he'd examined the contents until he found a thin common thread that bound the women together.

According to their medical records, each had recently broken a habit but couldn't remember how. Two of the women's agenda planners were missing a page from four consecutive weeks, but different months. One woman's daily journal also had a page torn from four consecutive weeks. To him, it looked as if they were hiding appointments or had been somewhere they didn't want others to know about. But why? Did these voids have anything to do with the crimes? Each had occurred a month prior to burglarizing their respective bank. Had these women done something for four weeks in a row that contributed to their crime? Why else would the information have been removed from their personal records? The folded business card he'd found tucked in the fourth woman's grocery coupons located in an empty pocket planner, caught and held his attention.

Flipping the business card between his fingers as he sipped his wine, he stared aimlessly at it. The word *thin* flashed behind his eyes. And by thin, he knew he didn't have enough evidence to report to his boss that would prove their connection. Yet his idea warranted further investigation, and tomorrow he planned to locate and observe the good doctor's practice. Before he left work, he'd researched Kalil Sayyad Riyad and found nothing. The man didn't exist. Not finding anything piqued Nolan's curiosity. Was the man a ghost, a plant by a terrorist group? He'd placed a request for an in-depth trace into the man's background on the desk of his colleague, Francis Finkelstein. If anyone could find information on a ghost, Finkelstein could and would. Nolan planned to call him first thing in the morning.

"Make it a true daily double, Alex."

Pete's voice snapped him from his thoughts. He laughed at his pet. Nolan stood, gulped the last of his wine, and then tossed Pete a treat from the bag he kept in the end table drawer. He set the DVR to play the show again for Pete.

"Don't stay up all night watching TV, pal." He rubbed Pete's head. "I'm going to bed."

"Goodnight, Nolan."

"Goodnight, Pete."

Chapter Four

Located in a single story row of shops and offices in the busy downtown shopping district, the office hadn't been hard to find. Briefcase in hand, Nolan walked along the sidewalk, stopped and pretended to straighten his hat in the window's reflection, then continued to the corner and crossed to the café. Thick drapes covered the large front windows, making it impossible to see inside. Immediately, his trained eyes located the topnotch security system around the windows and door. A small sign printed on the glass stated the purpose of the office and the address, but nothing else. No name or office hours appeared on the windows or door.

Hypnosis

Healthier Living Through Inner Strength

492 Duckard Street

Nolan took a seat in the sidewalk café across from the doctor's office. Numerous shoppers and commuters made his cover easy. He chose a perfect table at an angle to the left of the office and out of direct view of the windows or door. A row of hedges ran along the sidewalk, separating the walkway from the outdoor area of the café. Nolan ordered coffee and set up his laptop to make it look as if he were working. In reality, he was. The café's Wi-Fi connectivity gave him access to Francis and whatever he found.

One glance around and he knew his cover was safe. People clad in business attire ate breakfast as they tapped away on computers, cell phones, or other handheld devices. Assured that he blended well, Nolan settled into surveillance mode.

At ten a.m. sharp, a gentleman and a woman walked to the hypnotist's office. The man carried a white medical box. Nolan noted the direction from which they came, but hadn't seen them get out of a car. In a series of quick snaps, he took as many pictures as possible with a high-definition mini-camera. The moment they entered the building and closed the door, he connected the camera to the computer and uploaded the pictures to Francis to help aid in the couple's identification. When the upload completed, he unhooked the camera and returned it to his inside coat pocket. Within minutes, his cell phone rang.

"O'Connell here," Nolan stated, recognizing Finkelstein's number.

"Morning, Nolan. I take it the pictures you sent me are of this Riyad character."

"That's what I'm betting."

"Got in at five this morning. Been searching everything for your Kalil Sayyad Riyad. Nothing so far, but with the pictures I'm certain it's only a matter of time before we get a hit. I'm uploading the pictures to the international terrorists' database to search its files as well. Sooner or later, we'll know who he is. Any chance you could lift a fingerprint?"

Nolan couldn't stop the smile from splitting his face. Francis was the only member of his coworkers who knew his secret. Before joining the Treasury Department, Nolan had trained to be a CIA agent. What kid didn't want to be a spy? He snorted at the memory. With his master's degrees in business finance and law, the Treasury Department wanted him more. Besides, being undercover for months at a time didn't truly appeal to him. He repositioned in his seat as he stared at the office across the street. Being a Treasury Agent gave him the power to fight the bad guys where it hurt—in their pocketbooks.

Follow the money, seize the assets, shut them down, and stop the crime. Nolan liked taking down terrorists. He'd made a game out of finding their hidden bank accounts and watching for any illegal activity that constituted seizing their profits. It thrilled him to the core each time he heard of another criminal losing it all. Having the added spy training gave him an edge.

"I'll see what I can do." Before Nolan disconnected the call, he gave the coded message that let Francis know he'd be sitting surveillance on this guy. "I'm working out of the office today. Keep me informed if anything changes."

This detail of the job he liked. Standard procedure granted him permission to gather evidence using any means possible when dealing with a potential terrorist. Legal channels required a search warrant. In order to obtain a search warrant, he needed more evidence on this man than he had. No judge would grant him a warrant based on a folded business card, a series of missing pages from personal agenda books, and a gut instinct. No, what he needed was to get inside that office and locate plausible evidence to back his theory . . . with or without a warrant.

The door to the office opened and the pair walked out, shutting and locking the door behind them. Odd, they hadn't been in there long and they no longer carried the white medical box. A quick glance at his watch revealed approximately ten minutes had passed from the moment of entry to exit. Thinking of the security system, he didn't doubt his ability to bypass it and enter. He watched as they strolled to the far end of the street and turned the corner. He assumed they'd parked around the block due to limited spaces on Duckard Street. Or they didn't want their vehicle seen, just as he hadn't when he'd parked on the next street over.

In a casual conversation with his waitress, he learned she hadn't noticed the hypnotist's office maintaining set hours. In her opinion, they seemed to come and go, on and off, during her shift. Nolan finished the coffee and returned the laptop to his briefcase. Luck might be on his side. The pair had come and gone. Did that mean they wouldn't be back today?

Nolan casually crossed the street and strolled past the office. The drapes were still closed tight. Offices and shops ran the length of Duckard Street. At the corner, he turned and spotted an alleyway. The alley separated the buildings on Duckard from the buildings on the street that paralleled behind it. No doubt the majority of deliveries on the two streets were made via this passage. A few loading docks bustled with activity as he strolled along as if he belonged there. With everyone busy at work, no one seemed to take notice of him.

The florist shop next to the hypnotist's office had a sign that helped with locating the correct rear entrance. A plain, solid gray metal door marked the posterior doorway. He set his briefcase on the ground beside the door and slipped a hand into his inside coat pocket. The small specialty tools were a gift from Great-Uncle Floyd, the black sheep of the family. Rumor had it there wasn't a lock the man couldn't pick. Many summers ago, Nolan had spent time at his grandmother's house in the mountains and worked at Great-Uncle Floyd's hardware store.

"Never know when the tricks of the trade might come in handy," the words of Floyd whispered in his head. He smiled at the memory of where he'd learned the secret skill of breaking and entering. Palming the tools, he made quick work of the lock and returned the items to the thin leather pouch he kept inside his inner jacket pocket. This ability he never mentioned when he was hired. The Bureau would probably frown on such actions. Driven by gut instinct, determination set in as he checked the door for signs of a security system. *Odd.* He pursed his brows. The door had none.

Slowly, he opened the gray door just far enough to peek inside. A small alcove greeted his gaze. Nolan slung the strap of his briefcase over his head and across his shoulder for easier carrying, and then stepped inside, shutting the door. Another locked door blocked his entrance. This one came equipped with a primary security system. Nolan snorted at the crude setup. He bypassed it, then acknowledged they were smarter than he'd given them credit. A secondary, more complicated system had been installed. This one took a few minutes, but he managed to reroute the system. Gratitude for the detailed training he'd received washed over him as he opened the door and the system didn't trigger blaring alarms.

Nolan smiled and stepped inside the dark office. Slipping his hand into the side pocket of his briefcase, he pulled out a small flashlight and switched it on. Deliberately, he worked his way down the narrow hall. He opened a door—a bathroom. Past that, he entered the front of the office and the waiting area. Dim light entered around the thick drapes, but not enough to see anything. A reception desk sat beside a door across the room. A couch was positioned beneath the front window with a coffee table in front of it. On the opposite side of the reception desk was a water cooler complete with plastic cups.

He crossed to the desk then opened and shut each drawer. No paper, no files, no pens or paperclips—completely empty drawers. On a whim, he picked up the telephone receiver. No dial tone. No calls coming in or going out. He sighed. A definite front for something. But what?

Entering the door to the left of the reception desk, he located the exam room. In the corner sat a scale. A couple of potted plants, another thick shaded window, a wooden, Old World crafted desk and a high-back leather chair came into view. A comfortable looking chaise lounger sat in the center of the room with a small, wooden, round table beside it. Under that table sat a trash can containing three plastic cups. Nolan carefully gathered the used cups, placed them in baggies from his briefcase, and tucked them into a center pocket next to his laptop. So nothing looked disturbed, Nolan returned to the water cooler, grabbed three cups from the stack, then dropped them in the trash in the exam room.

Satisfied, he smiled. When he wrote his report, he'd simply state the cups were recovered from the suspect's trash. The minor detail of inside or outside garbage he planned to leave out.

Searching the exam room desk, he found nothing in any of the open drawers. The large bottom left-hand drawer was locked. Within a second, he mastered the lock and opened the drawer. It contained two gas masks and the white medical box. Inside that, he located vials of a lavender colored powder. Noting the presence of gas masks and not being sure what the powder was, he didn't open it. If he took one, would it be noticed? Deciding not to blow the investigation by tipping off the enemy, he put it back. He took pictures of the vial, its contents, and the case. About to shut the drawer, he noticed a folded piece of paper tucked between the box and the inside wall of the drawer.

Nolan spread the paper on the desk. He couldn't believe his eyes. A neatly written list of names ran dead center down the paper. Four names he recognized immediately, but the others he'd have to investigate. He snapped several pictures of the paper, then returned it to its former position. Making sure everything was how he'd found it, Nolan turned to leave. The click of the front door lock echoed in the dead silence of the office.

He froze. With no way out, his only option was to hide.

Amelia needed more information before continuing her sessions with Dr. Riyad. She called in and took a personal day. Now, not believing what she was doing, she stood in Dr. Riyad's office praying they wouldn't read the nervousness in her face. It wasn't like her to confront a doctor about his credentials, but in this case her gut instinct urged her to do so. Maybe the endless afternoons she'd played detective with her six brothers influenced her suspicious mind. They'd teased her mercilessly when she'd followed in their mother's footsteps and became an accountant and not a detective on the police force like their dad and them. She bit back a smile, knowing they'd be proud of her for following up on a *suspicious* character. But was he? She glanced from Dr. Riyad to Mina. Was she overreacting?

Hours on the Internet neither gave her insight nor eased her suspicions about Dr.

Riyad and the practice of hypnosis. She intended to drop in unannounced at his office and hopefully run into another patient. If she saw at least one other patron of the doctor's, it might ease her doubt a smidgeon. That hope dissipated the moment she parked and ran into them on the street.

A short conversation between her and the doctor brought them to the office. Dr. Riyad wished to discuss her concerns within the privacy of his office. Glancing around, the dark room gave her the creeps instead of the normal soothing sensation. Even when they flipped on the lights, it didn't subside. The whole situation didn't feel right, but she couldn't back out now. The need to know outweighed the wave of uncertainty crashing through her.

She took a deep breath, gathered her courage, and forced her legs to function as she followed him through the reception area into his exam room. Mina stayed in the reception area and closed the door. He beckoned her to sit in the recliner while he settled behind his desk. Instead of relaxing into the cushy comfort, she sat spine straight on the edge and faced him. This had to be the hardest thing she'd ever done, but she refused to back down and not discuss her concerns. Before he could speak, she powered through with her first question.

"Dr. Riyad, have any of your other patients suffered nightmares after starting your sessions?"

"Nightmares," Dr. Riyad repeated in a tone she knew was meant to calm her, but it didn't. "Not that I have heard. What sort of nightmares plague you?"

Her mother was a mild-mannered woman who believed it was best to avoid confrontation, accept things for what they were, and not attempt to change them. She wouldn't approve of Amelia questioning a doctor's abilities. Amelia closed her eyes for a moment and gathered her resolve. She didn't want to accept being slightly overweight and not change it. That was why she was here. The hypnosis worked. She'd shed some of the unwanted poundage. But was she justified in her worries over her job, hypnosis, and these nightmares?

"I . . ." She paused as she focused on the privacy screen in the far corner behind Dr. Riyad. Was that a dark-brown eye peeping out at her through the fold of the screen? No, it couldn't be. She licked her lips and continued. "I see visions of people, but I can't recognize them. They speak to me."

"What do they say?"

"I don't know." Funny, she thought she saw movement behind the screen. She blinked. Her eyes had to be playing tricks on her.

"Maybe these dreams were triggered by your change in diet. Have you eaten anything different lately? It's a known fact certain foods can incite unusual dream states."

She didn't get the chance to look again. Dr. Riyad's change in tone snapped her back to him. Was he talking down to her? Making her concerns insignificant by blaming them on food? That wouldn't do. She might occasionally lean on food for comfort, but these dreams had nothing to do with a change in diet. Amelia swallowed hard, choked back her sudden spike of anger, and plowed forward, determined to understand the nuances of hypnosis and the possible side effects or at least make the doctor sympathize with her symptoms.

"These dreams are like none I've ever had in my life. I envision people, but can't see their faces. Their images are blurry. Their voices mumble undecipherable commands. It's as if they're telling me to do something, but I can't remember what I'm supposed to do." She paused. Should she continue? Had she imagined the narrowing of his irises? Dr.

Riyad shifted in his seat. Was he uncomfortable? And if so, why? Was it because she didn't accept his explanation or was it something else? Instead of her suspicions abating, they escalated. Amelia couldn't help but study his posture. If she'd learned anything from her oldest brother Jacob, it was the fact body language spoke volumes. And in this case, Dr. Riyad's body screamed deception, keeping her on edge and alert.

He cleared his throat, his tone softened. "I've upset you. I didn't mean to. Hypnosis affects each individual differently. Perhaps we've awakened a dormant occurrence in your life. A past experience you've subconsciously suppressed because it's too painful to remember. We could investigate this with further sessions." A broad smile split his lips, showing sparkling white teeth.

The hair on the back of her neck stood on end. Something in his gaze struck her as dishonest. The twitch beneath his right eye confirmed it in her mind. A slight movement in the corner made her glance its way, confirming her suspicions that someone hid behind the screen. Why? Was it another client wanting answers just like she? Or . . . was it a burglar? It took great effort not to show fear or surprise as she returned her gaze to Dr. Riyad. Staring at him, she decided not to say a word about the intruder. Nope, she had another plan for that individual.

She spoke as calmly as possible. "Perhaps you're right, Dr. Riyad." Gathering her purse, she stood and held out her hand to him.

When he stood and took her hand, the need to leave rippled through her gut. For some reason, she knew she had to help whoever hid behind that screen. If they were desperate enough to break in and hide, then she wanted to know why. What had the doctor done to them? And what had the doctor done to her while under hypnosis? She wasn't buying that repressed memory bit. But how was she going to get the doctor and Mina out of the office so this person could escape?

"Thank you so much for your time. We can continue this during our regular scheduled session." Amelia hoped she sounded normal. "I'm sorry to have interrupted you and Mina. You were obviously on your way somewhere when I bumped into you."

She forced a smile and prayed he bought it. Slow and easy, she released the breath she held when he let go of her hand and stepped around the desk, guiding her toward the door.

"Are you sure you're okay? I can have Mina postpone the meeting we're scheduled to attend." The touch of his hand to the small of her back reinforced her desire to leave and countered his well-meaning speech. Obviously, the good doctor intended to follow her out the door.

"I'm fine. Again, I'm sorry to have bothered you." Amelia wasn't surprised when

Mina stood and followed them to the front door. "I greatly appreciate your time. See you on Friday."

"It was no inconvenience, Amelia." He dug into his inside suit pocket, pulled out a business card, and handed it to her. "Please feel free to contact me at any hour with your concerns. My cell phone number is on the bottom."

"Thank you, Doctor." She turned and nodded at the receptionist. "Have a great day, Mina."

Since they were parked near her car and would probably notice she hadn't left, she quickly added, "I think I'll do some shopping while I'm out. It's such a nice day to have off."

"Enjoy," Mina replied with a timid smile.

Amelia stepped out the door. They didn't immediately follow. A knot tightened in her gut. What should she do? Maybe they waited for her to leave. Nonchalantly, she turned and walked several shops away. She ducked into the dress shop and browsed the racks near the window. It seemed like an eternity passed before the doctor and Mina strolled by. Releasing her breath, Amelia walked from the shop, made sure they were gone and then returned to the office. A quick jiggle confirmed it was locked. On a whim, she hurried to the window outside the session room.

She took a deep breath and hoped this worked. One, two, three, she tapped hard on the glass. Nothing. Glancing around, she made sure no one watched then did it again. One, two, three. At the sight of the edge of the curtain lifting just enough for a brown eye to peek out at her, she froze. Something about that sensual soft-colored eye sent a thrill to her core. It belonged to a male and she knew it.

To be on the safe side, she shot a quick glance from side to side and hoped no one saw him or noticed what she was about to do. She pointed at him then to herself and gave a nod toward the café across the street. Holding her hand where only he could see, she flashed five fingers at him, letting him know she expected him to meet her in five minutes. Time seemed to stand still as she stared at the eye and it stared back at her. Then he did the unexpected which made her heart skip a beat. The curtain opened just far enough to see his face. With a touch of his hand to the brim of his hat and a quick nod, the curtain dropped and he was gone.

* * * *

Why had he let the woman see him? The lilt of her voice touched a soft spot, igniting a curiosity he couldn't deny. Nolan had to see the woman attached to the alluring tone. One quick peek was all it was supposed to be. He'd lingered from the moment he caught sight of her sitting taut on the edge of the chaise lounger until she spotted him. Every ounce of training screamed at his stupidity, but something in her eyes reassured him he was safe.

Never had anyone located him when undercover. It was a trait the CIA superiors loved about him and wanted to capitalize on if he had remained with them. His ability to blend with his surroundings and not be seen made him valuable. They claimed it was a priority asset for a good spy. If they could see him now, letting a mere civilian spot him, would they still feel the same? Nolan swallowed hard against the sudden lump in his throat. Why? Why had he let her see him?

It was a perplexed situation he couldn't figure out. At first sight, she'd stolen his breath and he couldn't help but stare. Long ebony curls made his fingers itch to twine those silken strands between them. Skin the color of fine porcelain, natural red full lips, and a body of a goddess piqued his interest. Those bright green eyes of hers caught and held his stare. Unable to blink for fear of missing one single feature of her beauty, Nolan had frozen and waited for a sign from this mysterious beauty. Would she turn him in or keep his secret?

When she didn't reveal his presence, he had to meet her. Part of him felt ashamed for listening in on her private doctor-patient conversation. But the agent part of him gathered every ounce of information possible to use against the doctor should he turn out to be a member of a terrorist sect. Riyad called her Amelia. She had to be the Amelia Morris listed on the paper he saw in the desk. Who was she and why was she a client of a hypnotist? The doctor mentioned her eating habits. No, it couldn't be her weight. From what he could see, there wasn't a thing wrong with her. She was perfect.

The moment she stood, he got the impression she was trying to help him. Listening closely, he picked up on the fact that the doctor seemed to be on his way out as well. Good. He sighed. His chance to escape had just been handed to him. Seconds ticked by that seemed like hours until the doctor and his assistant left. Like any good agent, he waited until he was certain it was safe to leave unnoticed. He got to the doorway between the session room and the reception area when he was stopped in his tracks.

Tap, tap, tap echoed in the room behind him. Nolan turned and looked toward the window. Uncertain what he should do, he remained still, listening for any disturbance. Another tap, tap, tap rattled his nerves. Though he knew he should ignore it and leave, he couldn't. Like a moth drawn to the light, he eased to the window and slowly lifted the edge of the curtain just enough to peek out.

The beautiful woman named Amelia stood staring back at him. *This shouldn't be happening*, he reprimanded himself. He shouldn't have blown his cover. If he'd left it as it was, she'd probably come to the conclusion she'd been seeing things. Something deep inside controlled his motions and made him respond. With a nod of his head and a touch of his hat, he agreed to meet with her at the café.

Nolan spotted Amelia seated at a corner table in the front courtyard of the café. He'd sensed her gaze on him the moment he crossed the street and headed in her direction. Curiosity and a hint of nervousness shone in her eyes. Did she realize how dangerous it was to meet a complete stranger like this? Especially one she'd spotted hiding in her doctor's office. Anger churned in his gut that she'd take such a risk.

What was she thinking?

Chapter Five

Amelia caught sight of the man the moment he turned the corner. She knew it was him. Out of the few gentlemen wearing hats, his was the most distinctive. He walked tall, shoulders straight, chin lifted, and had an air about him that kick-started her heart. The sun at his back helped the hat shadow his features as he headed in her direction, setting her imagination on full throttle. She knew he had sexy brown eyes. But what else? He'd kept his features from view behind the office curtain. With each step he took, her heartbeat increased and her mouth dried in anticipation.

Oh God! What would she say? She hadn't thought this through, simply acted on impulse. Dropping her hands from the table, she knotted the napkin in her lap as he got closer. *Breathe, just breathe. Sit straight, show no fear, and be direct in your questioning.* The words she'd overheard between her father and one of her brothers resurfaced in her head. Swallowing hard, she lifted her shoulders, tilted her chin, and met the hidden gaze of the approaching stranger. Though every ounce of her insides shook, she prayed he wouldn't notice her nervousness.

Dressed in a gray suit, white shirt, and a gray tie, she assumed him to be a business man. A messenger-style bag hung across his body at his right hip. The tan cowboy hat added a defiant sort of flair. It blended and yet it didn't. *A rebel at heart.* The thought made her lips itch to smile, but she managed to swallow it. She forced what she hoped appeared as a cool façade. From her seated position, she guesstimated him to be around six feet. Much taller than her five-foot-two. *Tall, lean, and*—the moment he stood across from her at the table, he removed his hat and it was all she could do not to let her jaw drop—

handsome. More than handsome in her book. Something about the boyish freckles made her want to play connect-the-dots with kisses. The way the sunlight graced his hair brought out the wonders of his gorgeous red waves. Never had she even thought that a man would look so delectable with such a phenomenal shade of hair. Yet, he did. She couldn't help but smile when she met the dark-brown gaze of what she deduced as a perfect male specimen. Now if he had an ounce of intelligence behind those sexy eyes, he'd be a gift from heaven.

No, screamed through her head, squelching her rampant libido to a halt. He's a stranger she'd caught hiding in Dr. Riyad's office. For the life of her, she couldn't understand why she hadn't turned him in. Or for that matter, why she'd tapped on that window and arranged this meeting. Oh God! She forced her gaze to remain level with his. What sort of trouble had she gotten herself into now? She wasn't her brothers. She didn't have their law enforcement training.

"We seem to have met under unusual circumstances. My name is Nolan O'Connell."

She liked the sound of his voice. Smooth as silk in a mid-baritone range, which made her hunger to have him whisper sweetly in her ear. It was all she could do to refrain from visibly shivering at the thought of his warm breath tickling the tender skin of her ear. His hand hovered in mid-air for several long seconds before she finally accepted it.

A strong masculine hand wrapped around hers with a grip that would make her father and brothers proud. They'd often said one could tell a lot about a man through his grip. Staring straight into his eyes, Amelia sensed a deep inner strength within his core. His touch warmed her skin, sending bolts of heat up her arm, causing goosebumps to cascade down her spine. Never had she reacted this way to anyone's touch.

But now wasn't the time for this. She needed to know what this man named Nolan was up to and why. Not sure what to do, she remembered her father saying *the best way to learn the truth was to be straightforward and ask.* Gathering her resolve, she forced a calm to her voice that she definitely didn't feel inside.

"I'm Amelia Morris and I'd like to know what you were doing hiding in Dr. Riyad's office and why?"

To her surprise a smile upturned his lips, adding a sexy charm to his face. She hated to admit the man was hot. Just looking at him spiked her libido into overdrive.

"May I sit?"

She heard him ask the question while she simply stared, wide-eyed at his sensual smile. All she could do was nod. Amelia forced her gaze to the hat he laid in the chair to her left. What was wrong with her? She swallowed hard. This had to stop. She had to not think about how hot and sexy this man appeared to be and think only of where she'd first seen him—Dr. Riyad's office hiding behind the privacy screen.

Then it struck her. Had he heard their conversation? Did he pay attention to her innermost fears about being hypnotized and the ensuing string of strange dreams? He must think her a kook. But he was the one hiding in the office, she reminded herself. That didn't make him any different than she. Other than he may have been there to rob the place.

Eyeing him up and down, she decided, petty criminals didn't dress in expensive suits or wear sexy cowboy hats. He hadn't been there to commit a burglary. It had to be an alternative motive. One she intended to find out. Before he could ask her anything she sat back taut, chin tilted, and gaze leveled on his.

"Mr. O'Connell, I'll ask again." She paused, licked her lips, and watched his face for clues. "Why were you hiding in Dr.

Riyad's office?"

Soft skin had met his hand in a firm, confident grip. He liked that. A woman with a decent handshake. Most merely did a brief, weak-wristed touch, but not her. She firmly clasped his hand. Heat filtered from her palm to his, sending a new wave of desire to war with his intellect. Nolan forced their hands to separate as he struggled to maintain a professional attitude and not one of a horny stalker on the prowl.

Nolan read the indecision in her eyes. She wasn't thinking past the knock on the window. He sensed her nervousness even though she tried desperately to portray a calm, cool, and collected woman. He didn't buy it. Those gorgeous, vivid green eyes spoke the truth. Meeting strange men wasn't her normal, especially ones she'd caught being bad. He swallowed the smile that threatened to split his lips. There were things he needed to know about this woman.

From the agent standpoint, he should ask why she was a patient of Dr. Riyad? Was she simply a patient or a partner in some sort of twisted scheme? The male libido wanted to take a different approach entirely. *Are you married? Dating? Will you go out with me?* Nolan froze. Where had those questions come from? He didn't have time for a relationship.

Looking at her, part of him wanted nothing more than to ask her out. She was the most beautiful woman he'd ever seen. Something about her stirred to life a spark he thought had died when his college girlfriend stomped his heart flat by dumping him to marry a rich tycoon's son. When he'd first joined TFI, a small portion of him hoped to find a dirty money trail on that particular businessman and dash her dreams of fortune. But the rich playboy did it to her himself with a black market scandal that landed him in prison. He shook the thought of his last disastrous try at love from his head. This meeting wasn't about dating. It pertained to gaining information on a possible terrorist suspect. Nothing more. Half-heartedly he tried to convince himself of that.

When he'd removed his hat, he caught the flash of a momentary approving gaze that reassured his male ego she liked what she saw. At least that's what he secretly hoped even though he tried to deny it.

Nolan couldn't help the smile. He truly liked her moxie. Straight forward questions, distinctive air of being in control even though he read a swirl of nervous emotions beneath her exterior. The perfect woman created for him sat across the table and he couldn't act upon his desires and ask her on a date. No, he was working and until further notice, she was a possible lead in this investigation. Nothing more, nothing less.

Soaking in her beauty, he hoped he was wrong. Twice she'd asked him what he was doing in the doctor's office. He needed an answer but his mind had bogged down with thoughts of Amelia. He ran a hand through his hair and noted her gaze followed his every move. If he hadn't read it wrong, he swore he saw a spark of sensual heat in her eyes. *Stop it*, he reprimanded himself. This woman wasn't his to fantasize about. What if she turned out to be a suspect? Where would that leave a relationship? *Relationship*, again with that insufferable word. He battled the urge to roll his eyes. He didn't even know her.

Taking a deep breath, he redirected his thoughts and focused on the conversation and not the fullness of her voluptuous lips. He delved into his trove of training and came up with what he believed to be a plausible excuse for his presence in that room.

"I'm a client. I have issues with . . ." He deliberately paused, leaned closer to her across the table, shot a quick glance around, then continued in a whispered tone. "I'm a businessman with a strong desire to pick locks. It's a problem the good doctor claims he can cure. I dropped by to see him. The office was locked so I let myself in. I didn't expect him to come in with another client so I hid, embarrassed that I'd be caught doing the one thing I wanted his help to rectify."

Amelia leaned forward as well. Something in her eyes suggested she wasn't buying it, even though she asked, "Do you steal anything after you pick locks?"

"No, I just like opening things that are locked, be it a door, a safe, whatever." He shrugged, sitting erect. The woman intrigued him. What was her game?

"Then what's the problem if you don't take anything?"

"I'm afraid that one day I might."

"I guess that's a justifiable reason." The slight smile that touched her lips had him staring at her mouth. "Did you let Dr. Riyad know you were there after I left?"

"No." He shook his head, hoping to clear

the sudden need to taste her mouth. "I was too embarrassed. I waited for them to leave. I was on my way out when you knocked on the window."

"Why'd you answer if you were in the free and clear to escape? I was the only one who saw you and I didn't get a look at your face, just one eye."

Her question made sense. Why did he? For a split second he considered his reasons, but drew a blank. He hated leading her on and not telling her exactly who and what he was. But he couldn't. Not until he learned the truth about her. Every ounce of him wanted desperately to clear her name and extinguish any possible connection with the hypnotist. Especially if it turned out the man was a terrorist.

Instead of answering, he fired several questions point blank. "Why didn't you turn me in? You could've said something. Why didn't you? And better yet, why'd you tap on the window?"

Amelia's mouth dropped open for a second as if she would speak, but didn't. She sat back, closed her mouth, and sifted through her reasoning. Never had she been this bold. Why didn't she turn him in? No matter how hard she thought about it, she didn't have an answer. Something in her gut had led her to make that decision.

"I'm not sure why I didn't." She held a level gaze on him. The warmth in his eyes soothed her unease and helped give her the confidence to continue. It suddenly didn't matter how she'd met him. Instantly, she wanted to learn more about him and help him in any way she could. Even if she sensed he hid the truth. "You're probably going to think I'm crazy, but I read something in your gaze that asked me not to."

Nolan reached across the table and took her hands in his. "I don't think you're crazy. I'm grateful you didn't say anything. How about I buy you lunch and the two of us get to know one another, not as clients of Dr. Riyad but as possible friends?"

"I think that would be a fine idea."

She wasn't sure why she agreed. Part of her was ecstatic over the opportunity to learn more about this handsome stranger. After all, they were in a very public place, so she knew she was safe. The other part of her warned he wasn't being entirely truthful and it would probably be best if she left. On a heavy sigh, she shrugged, realizing she wasn't being entirely honest with him either. There was no way she intended to explain her reasoning for being a client, even if he did ask.

"Here's to forming new friendships." He motioned for a waitress.

* * * *

Several days earlier, their lunch had lasted into the late afternoon. Once the conversation changed from how they'd met to learning more about each other, the time had flown.

Amelia couldn't believe she'd agreed to have dinner with him on Saturday night. It wasn't like her to give her personal cell phone number to a man she'd just met. But she did and it thrilled her to the core to know he had it. They'd spoken twice since then. Once, Nolan called just to say hello. The second time, he called to confirm their date, the time and place where he should pick her up.

In between images of a hot, red-headed Irishman with sexy freckles and a heart-stopping smile, nightmares plagued her. Amelia tossed and turned, then finally gave up trying to sleep. The long bubble bath and glass of red wine before bed hadn't helped. She sat upright, plumped the pillow, and leaned against the headboard, staring into the darkness. Several nights in a row she'd had the same terrifying nightmare. Vague images danced in her head. The distinct sensation of having to do something gripped her soul. But what? What did she have to do?

Thrashing a hand through her hair, she tried to calm her nerves. The dreams were getting worse, more controlling. Amelia sorted through her twisted thoughts, listing the when and why these nightmarish episodes started. If memory served her correctly, the dreams began after her first session. Had Dr. Riyad tapped into a hidden memory in her subconscious through hypnosis as he suggested?

No. She shook her head. She doubted there were any diabolical memories buried. Having grown up with six older brothers who protected her every move, nothing bad had ever happened to her. They made sure of it. Amelia sighed heavily. No, these dreams pertained to something else. No matter what the good doctor wanted her to believe, her gut instinct suggested otherwise. That, plus meeting the handsome Nolan O'Connell spurred her suspicions behind the truth of his strange visit to Dr. Riyad's office.

She was certain he wasn't a client of the hypnotist as claimed. Something about him didn't add up. Every now and then during their conversation, he'd randomly asked odd questions about her relationship with Dr. Riyad. She sensed there was more to Nolan's persona than he let on and she intended to find out every nuance about the sexy man. Whether Nolan meant to or not, he had increased her concerns about completing her appointments with the hypnotist. Should she or shouldn't she?

A knot tightened in her chest as anxiety brewed. She hadn't thought about the sanctity of her job when she started these sessions. All she'd wanted was to lose unwanted pounds. Nolan's statement of concern over the possibility of losing his job if they found out about his lock-picking addiction started her thinking of her position.

Had she spilled any secrets? This fear surmounted all others. She loved her job. As accountants for the United States Mint, she and Louisa both held a high security clearance at the United States Bullion Depository. They kept and maintained detailed logs of every item within those vaults. Quarterly, they inventoried different sections, one of which was due within the next few weeks.

The average accountant's life consisted of crunching boring numbers and doing taxes, but hers was far more enjoyable. Few got the opportunity she had to keep the records of the United States' gold reserve and its indescribable secrets. Her heart swelled with pride. Amelia pulled the covers to her chest. Was she overreacting to these dreams? Were they nothing more than just nightmares? Louisa seemed to think they didn't mean anything. But Nolan had shown a true interest. He'd questioned her about the conversation he'd overheard between her and Dr. Riyad. Their detailed discussion continued to stir her curiosity and doubts at the same time. Why was Nolan interested in her odd dreams? The one thing that bothered her most . . . had she spilled something to Dr. Riyad about her job that could get her fired?

The whole thing was making her jittery and more suspicious of everything. Just the other day, she bumped into the janitor, Hubert, coming out of her office and was almost certain he'd been through her desk drawers. After finding nothing missing but the garbage from her can, she realized how far this growing anxiety controlled her. She had even sworn Hubert was following her around the workplace. Louisa suggested she was simply noticing him more because Terrence had spoken about him and told her the man's name. Still, Amelia couldn't shake the feeling something was not right with that man.

Amelia shivered. As Louisa had claimed, it *was* probably all the healthy deli food they'd been consuming over the past week causing these dreams to worsen. She couldn't help but smile as she remembered that chat. Their lunch with Terrence hadn't been awful like she'd expected. He'd been astonishingly fun and personable, making jokes about the health food while they ate. They'd enjoyed his company so much the three of them became lunchtime pals. She hated to admit it, but he'd turned out to be likable. Instead of avoiding him, they'd managed friendly conversations when he'd made his rounds delivering the departmental mail.

But he wasn't Nolan. She sighed. Now, there was a man who excited her soul. Though she didn't know him well, she found him astonishingly attractive and hungered to see him again.

One glance at the clock showed she needed to make another attempt to sleep. Work came early and she had her third appointment with Dr. Riyad scheduled for late afternoon. She snuggled into her blankets, readjusted her pillow, and tried to focus on her favorite part of the job—inventory. It was the only time any section of the vault was opened. More than just gold rested within its walls. Few knew what she did, and as long as she lived she never planned to share that knowledge with anyone. Amelia closed her eyes and prayed for sleep.

Think of Nolan, a little voice whispered in the back of her head. Unable to stop the smile that tugged at her lips, she cuddled her pillow and sighed. The gorgeous image of Nolan's freckled face with the deep dimples when he smiled, the dark-brown eyes, and the sexy, red hair filtered into her thoughts, luring her into a comfort zone. Sleep finally came as she fantasized about tracing every freckle on his person with the tip of her tongue.

* * * *

The day after he visited Dr. Riyad's, Nolan and Francis set up a surveillance location in a vacant office situated across the street and two doors down from the suspect's office. Several days passed and no activity occurred. He'd managed to plant a bug in the session room, but no video equipment. At least they had ears. He and Francis took turns watching the place.

DNA and fingerprints from one of the cups came back as Amelia's. Somehow she'd taken root in Nolan's brain and refused to dissipate. A twinge of guilt tugged at his soul for reading the chart containing her profile. She lived in the Rosewood Apartments, was unmarried, had no children, and was a civilian accountant for the United States Mint assigned at Fort Knox. He'd nearly spewed his coffee when he discovered that tidbit of information. What made matters worse was another of the names on the list he'd found in the doctor's desk drawer. Louisa Langley also worked as an accountant at Fort Knox.

What did a so-called hypnotist want with two accountants employed at Fort Knox? The same thing he wanted with the other four ladies on his list—*money*. A knot formed in Nolan's gut at the idea his theory might be right. Someone was plotting to break into the impenetrable vault. Was Amelia in on it or simply a pawn in this madman's game? God, he hoped for the latter of the two scenarios. She was the first woman in years to intrigue him and taunt his dreams. He snorted as he continued to watch the office. He had a job to do, which didn't include getting involved with a possible suspect.

Finally, late Friday afternoon, Dr. Riyad and Mina returned. This time, Nolan spotted their vehicle and took photos of the license and car. When he sent the information to Francis, it came back as registered to a bogus corporation. Just like the office, a background check proved it was leased to a ghost company, which led them from one bogus account to another. Dr. Riyad's true identity was buried under a mountain of subterfuge.

Slipping out of the surveillance office,

Nolan attached a tracking device to the suspect's car and returned in a matter of minutes. Half an hour later, a small compact car pulled into a parking spot several car lengths behind the suspect's car. When the car door opened and a sexy, sandaled foot touched the ground, every ounce of him went rigid. Amelia slid from the driver's side, stood, then closed and locked the door.

Long, ebony curls hung below her shoulders. Oversized sunglasses hid what he knew were bright green eyes. For five-foot-two, she carried herself well. Dressed in a green summer dress and sensible low-heeled sandals, she looked stunning. When she turned and stared in his direction as if she'd seen him, Nolan lowered the binoculars. Unable to resist, he simply stared, soaking in every inch possible of her perfection.

She couldn't see him. Tinted, one-way glass had been installed in the front window when they moved in. Nonetheless, he sensed a connection between them. For a split second, he swore she smiled at him. The professional aspect of his brain sent a blow to his libido that kick-started his brain back to life, forcing him to re-focus. Was this beautiful woman a victim or a willing participant? He couldn't stop the question from repeatedly tormenting his thoughts. Deep down he leaned toward victim instead of criminal. The moment she walked into the hypnotist's office, Nolan hesitated before slipping on the headphones. Guilt flooded his system but he had to know.

Victim or suspect?

* * * *

Amelia hadn't slept well. Every time she'd closed her eyes the sensation of forgetting something cloaked her, making the nightmare return. In the early morning hours, a strange vision became clear, upsetting her even more. A fuzzy image of someone in a gas mask hovering over her caused her to wake with a start. Who was it and what were they trying to make her do? No matter how hard she concentrated, she couldn't understand the words they'd spoken. It was as if a portion of this nightmare remained hidden just out of reach of her thought pattern. Something prevented it from surfacing and that scared her. In her heart, she knew it wasn't a recessive event from her past.

If strange things were happening to her, were they also happening to Nolan? Had he suffered nightmares as well? Was that the real reason behind his impromptu visit to the doctor's office? Was he trying to uncover something the doctor didn't want known about his practice? An absurd plan formulated in her head as one scenario after another toyed with her thoughts. She had to know what occurred when she was under Dr. Riyad's hypnotic trance. Not remembering past the initial sound of his voice at the start of each session bothered her. What did he do to her? What did he say? Something provoked these nightmares and she needed to determine the catalyst. If not for her safety and sanity, then for her best friend, Louisa, and her hot new friend Nolan. There was no telling what the good doctor did to them as well.

Before arriving at the office, she visited an electronics store and bought a mini-recording device. Nerves wrenched her gut, but determination steeled her spine as she walked. If nothing else, she'd have a recording of their session. Taking off the sunglasses, she wished she could keep them on to hide the dark circles beneath her eyes. Inhaling deep, she prayed her nervousness didn't show. She tried desperately not to think of the device hidden in her purse.

For an instant, she focused on the memory of Nolan's image and it steadied her nerves. Odd, thinking of this new friend aided her determination to succeed at this little feat of espionage. The thought almost made her laugh, but she managed to suppress it. Nolan picked locks and she hid tape recorders in her purse. What a perfect pair they made...

Amelia frowned. Where'd that come from? They weren't a pair or a couple or anything other than new friends. It had to be these dreams making her so addled she'd grappled for any lifeline to hold onto for security. Nolan just happened to be that momentary lifeline and not the leading man in the next chapter of romance in her life. It couldn't be anything else.

Straightening her spine, she steadied her steps. As she stood in front of Mina's desk, she placed the sunglasses in her purse and pressed the record button. She hoped the kid at the store was right and this thing didn't make any detectable noises. He guaranteed it would record for a solid six hours straight. Not that she needed that long. Their sessions lasted only two hours.

"Hello, Miss Morris." Mina smiled. Her accent wasn't as difficult to understand as Dr.

Riyad's. Mina's head was covered with a traditional hijab and she wore a soft pastel-colored, full-length dress with long sleeves.

"Hello, Mina." Amelia forced her voice to sound normal even though her insides twisted.

"You are on time as always." Mina stood, walked to the exam room door, and opened it. "Come, let us weigh you, and check your progress."

Following Mina, Amelia walked to the scale and stepped on. This would be the deciding factor. Had she managed four pounds in a week? Her clothes felt like she had. The dress she wore was loose around the middle. The scale leveled off and her jaw dropped. *Five pounds.* She'd lost five instead of four for a total of ten pounds in three weeks. She couldn't believe it. Maybe she was wrong to mistrust Dr. Riyad. No, even if she were wrong, she'd have the tape to prove it.

"Dr. Riyad will be pleased," Mina stated.

"I can't believe it," Amelia said in awe.

"I've never dropped ten pounds with any diet, no matter how hard I tried."

"By the time your sessions are complete,"—Mina guided Amelia to the chaise lounger—"your goal has the potential to be reached."

Amelia settled into the seat and set her purse on the floor next to her as usual. She didn't want to do anything different to rouse suspicion, like keep it in her lap. Not wanting the recorder to miss anything that was said, she thought beside the chair was close enough.

Dr. Riyad entered dressed in a fine white, silk suit. It offset the tan of his skin, giving him an even darker complexion. He reminded her of an Arab sheik from the old silent movie era. All he lacked was the proper headgear and a horse. Mina shared the news of Amelia's successful weight loss.

"That is wonderful, Amelia." His thick accent rolled over her as he took his place in the chair facing her. "By the end of our final session you should be near your goal and your life changed forever on the weight loss path."

Life changed forever. What exactly did he mean by that? Was there an ominous message in his tone or was she overreacting out of fear for her job? Amelia breathed deeply, trying to quell her nerves as she gathered the courage to ask.

"Dr. Riyad, I have to ask you again about this. It's truly bothering me. Have any of your other patients suffered nightmares?"

His gaze seemed to darken and the look that passed between him and Mina fertilized her suspicions. He straightened in his chair as he returned his stare to her. Amelia held her gaze level on his. The tone of his voice sounded slightly agitated and concise more than that of concern. Obviously, something about this subject made him anxious. Maybe she shouldn't have asked before their session.

"Have your nightmares worsened, Amelia?"

"Yes . . ."

He cut her off with a series of quick questions. "Have you learned anything new from your nightmares? Can you describe them? What do you see when you dream?"

Amelia took a second to regain her composure and decided not to share the truth. The strange vibe she suddenly sensed from him made her ill-at-ease, but she did her best to hide it. Even though the image of someone hovering over her in a gas mask flashed inside her head, she kept it to herself. In as steady a tone as she could muster, she gave him the same answer she'd given him before. "That's the problem; they're just blurry images. Nothing is decipherable."

To her it looked as if relief brightened his face. She swallowed hard. Maybe this wasn't such a good idea. The hair on her arms prickled, warning something wasn't right with the situation. Every molecule of her being suggested she leave.

As if he read her indecision, he spoke in his normal calming tone. "Let us venture to say you may be experiencing a vision of something buried in your subconscious. Once we complete your weight loss sessions, together with hypnosis we can free your mind of the locks that hide it from you. That is if you so choose to learn these secrets. Some choose to be happy with the results of their initial sessions and go no further with the natural healing of one's mind. For now, let's continue with your path to weight loss success."

Dr. Riyad wasted no time. Before she had a chance to reconsider, he gathered her hand and began. Within seconds, she relaxed into the chaise, her eyes instantly closed as instructed, even though she battled to keep them open. He released her hand and she knew he moved to stand behind her. A familiar scent filled the air as Dr. Riyad urged her to breathe deep. Had his voice become muffled? Amelia strained to hear. If she had to name the fragrance, she couldn't. The only reason she recognized it, she'd smelled it during prior sessions. It must be some exotic incense or something he used to soothe his patients' nerves, she reasoned as lightheadedness took control. Lightheadedness. The word shot through her brain as she grappled to remain conscious, but couldn't.

Had he drugged her? Was that scent some sort of herbal drug? She struggled against the overwhelming sensation taking over her system. His voice led her into a fog, leaving her floating on a cloud under his control.

Nolan couldn't believe what he heard. After a few moments, he didn't hear Amelia, just Dr. Riyad. Though his gut instinct was to storm the office and save her, he forced himself to stay put. If anything, he wanted to clear Amelia's name. Why? From what? The questions sprang to life in his brain. Though he hated to admit it, he truly wanted to get to know the sexy, green-eyed beauty better.

Forcing his focus to the job, he repositioned the headphones and listened. From the gist of the conversation, he learned she visited the hypnotist for help with weight management. Nonsense. She carried a nicely rounded, fuller figure well in his opinion. His back straightened. Man, he needed to stop thinking of Amelia as a woman, but as a possible suspect. *Or a victim*, the little ounce of hope at the base of his brain whispered. The second choice he could rescue. The first he'd have to arrest.

Amelia's image wouldn't leave his thoughts no matter how hard he tried. He shook his head and continued listening to the conversation. He gathered something bothered Amelia. *Nightmares*. What sort of nightmares, she really didn't explain, but seemed to think they were connected to the hypnosis sessions.

Riyad came through loud and clear. He

seemed to be placing her into some sort of trance. Seconds later, he began giving her instructions. Riyad's voice changed. It sounded muffled as if . . . he wore a gas mask. The idea hit Nolan square between the eyes. There must be something about the powdered substance that made it airborne. Was it a drug Riyad used to control his victims? Nolan's jaw tightened and his abdominal muscles clenched at what Riyad told Amelia. Unfortunately, Nolan's theory proved to be right. Someone wanted access to the Fort Knox vaults. Every ounce of him burned to rush the office and arrest the man. But, he couldn't. Not yet. He needed more evidence, so he forced himself to do nothing but listen and continue to record with fists clenched at his sides.

Questions swirled. Had Riyad done the same thing to the women from the banks? Their names were on his list. Had they visited for help with some problem and been rewarded by him implanting commands? What had Riyad done with the money? Were he and Mina in this alone or were they a part of a larger terrorist organization? Nolan needed to know. He couldn't let that money leave the country. He paced and stared at the office across the street. The more he listened, the more heated his blood turned.

Riyad repeated the instructions over and over for at least twenty minutes. He wanted something from the vault and it wasn't money. The description of the object couldn't be misunderstood. Amelia had to enter the vault and locate the Sacred Diamond of Shabib. Nothing else—no gold, just get this diamond and leave. Nolan sat at the table and tapped the information into the search engine on his laptop as he continued to listen.

The Sacred Diamond of Shabib was a mythical object from a long forgotten desert tribe somewhere in Arabia. The story read it once belonged to Sheik Azir Hajeem Shabib.

It was rumored to contain a terrific power for the one who possessed it. Generation after generation, the ruling sheik protected the diamond until it disappeared in the late-eighteen hundreds. It was believed stolen and lost forever, leading to the end of Shabib's descendents tyrannical rule of the desert people.

Nolan's brows pursed. What made them think this fabled object was real and resided in Fort Knox? He knew the rumors that more than just gold was locked behind those walls. But no one knew for sure. *Maybe an accountant knew.* Nolan's eyes widened. Amelia Morris and Louisa Langley were both high-security clearance personnel for the United States Mint. If they knew secrets of the vault, it stood to reason they'd be targets for someone with a crazy idea about what lay hidden within.

He sat back in his chair. Why commit the bank thefts first? Where was the money?

Riyad stopped repeating the instructions, causing Nolan to refocus on listening. It sounded as if the doctor and his assistant had left the room. A door opened and closed in the background. Nolan picked up the binoculars and focused on the office. No one exited the front. Mumbled voices were heard through the listening device, but Nolan couldn't understand. With fine-tuning, the sound techs at the lab could pull the voices from the background and reproduce the conversation.

Forty-five minutes passed before anything tangible surfaced. Nolan heard the door open again. Riyad and Mina returned. At the sound of his voice, Nolan sat straight. The good doctor compelled Amelia to wake. Straining to hear, Nolan didn't relax until Amelia spoke. Why did it worry him? He didn't know her, but for some reason he needed to hear her voice and know she was all right.

The woman was a victim. That's why concern burned within him Nolan tried to convince himself. He didn't like what Riyad did to these women. If Amelia succeeded in stealing the diamond—if it even existed—then her life would permanently be altered. Just like Riyad proclaimed at the beginning of their session.

Life changed forever. Nolan ground his teeth. He had to stop this. Riyad would not ruin another woman's life; especially not Amelia's . . . not if he could help it.

Chapter Six

Amelia awoke, lightheaded and thirsty
again. A dry burn coated her throat. Fear
gripped her soul. Something didn't feel right.
In her heart, she knew she'd been drugged.
But how? Blurred images of two people in gas
masks traipsed through her head. Was the
scent she smelled a drug? Oh God! The
moment Dr. Riyad grasped her elbow, she
froze. Panic attempted to overwhelm her, but
she closed her eyes and steeled herself against
it. She could do this. All she needed to do was
get out of here without raising their suspicions
and listen to the recording to understand the
truth of what happened. If she could handle
six older brothers, she could fake-out one
crazed hypnotist. Inhaling deeply, she
attempted to appear calm and hoped he
couldn't read her thoughts.

"Are you okay?"

She opened her eyes and forced a fake smile to her lips. "May I have some water? I'm thirsty."

"Of course," Dr. Riyad replied.

Within seconds, Mina appeared with a cup. Amelia took it and drank it in one gulp. Though every ounce of her wanted to leap from the chair and run from the room, she managed to force herself to remain seated. In as normal a motion as she could, Amelia gathered her purse and stood. Lightheadedness threatened to crumple her knees, but she refused to buckle. Slowly, she turned to Dr. Riyad.

"Thank you." She didn't feel gratitude. Something inside urged she wasn't safe. Every fiber of her being screamed a warning. Her throat burned, the hair on her arms stood on end, and her stomach churned.

"I expect similar results next week." Dr. Riyad guided her toward the door.

"We'll see." Amelia tried to sound cheerful as she nodded.

"Same time next week?" Mina asked.

"Of course." Amelia turned and as casually as possible walked across the waiting room and out the front door.

The moment she stood in the sun, relief washed over her. In case they watched, she strolled to her car and got in, forcing herself not to rush. It wouldn't do to raise their suspicions. A quick glance in the rearview and she knew it was safe to pull into traffic. She couldn't wait to get home and listen to the recording. Once she turned off Duckard, she headed straight for home.

"Did you get all of that," Nolan stated in his call to Francis.

"Yep, every sick little bit of it. The team's in place, ready to take him down at your command."

"Wait and follow them, see where they lead us," Nolan replied. "If they don't come out of there with that white box, send in a hazmat team. I've got a feeling whatever that stuff is, it's airborne and dangerous."

"Roger that," Francis replied. "You coming?"

"Nope, I'm going after the victim. We're going to need her testimony."

Minutes after locking herself inside her apartment, the doorbell rang. Her heart skipped a beat. Had someone followed her? Was it that weird little Hubert? No. She tried to convince her racing pulse to slow. No one followed her, especially not him. This was just a coincidence. The moment she peeked through the peephole, she sensed it wasn't. A man in a gray suit wearing a tan, stylish cowboy hat stood outside her door.

Her jaw dropped. She managed to push past the solid lump in her throat as she opened the door. "Nolan?"

She couldn't believe he stood there. Sifting through her thoughts, she didn't remember inviting him over or giving him her address. Their date was for tomorrow night and she purposely suggested they meet at the restaurant. It was a habit she'd formed early in her dating life. Never give a guy your address until you're sure he's a decent person. One never knew what sort of kooks lurked in this world.

Looking him up and down, she wasn't sure if he was one of those kooks or a nice guy simply wanting to surprise her. He looked scrumptious in his business suit. A devilish portion of her itched to try on his hat and run her fingers through his hair. But one thing warred with her libido, keeping her system in check.

How'd he get her address?

Did he follow her after their lunch earlier in the week? Why show up now? Amelia shot a glance over her shoulder at the purse sitting on the coffee table. Desperately, she wanted to hear that tape. With him here, she couldn't.

How could she get him to leave?

"Amelia, I have a confession to make. I'm a Treasury Agent." He held a badge where she could read it. "And I need a moment of your time."

Trembling fingers reached for his badge, stating on a whisper she wanted a closer look. Seconds ticked by before she leveled her gaze on his and lifted her shoulders. Her voice cracked, mistrust riddled her words.

"What do you want?" He caught the badge she tossed at him before it hit the ground.

He leaned in close and lowered his voice. "It has to do with your visit to Dr. Riyad today." She gasped as he quickly added, "I'm sure you don't want your neighbors hearing our conversation. May I come in?"

Amelia hesitated, then stepped back and opened the door wider, allowing him inside. The moment the door closed he removed his hat and held it, rolling the brim nervously.

"Amelia . . ." She arched an eyebrow at

him, causing him to clear his throat and start over. "Miss Morris, I believe you've been the victim of a heinous crime."

"What?" she stuttered, stepping back. "What do you mean?"

"Dr. Riyad planned to steal from Fort Knox."

Oh God. Sickness swirled in her stomach. Her head spun. Nolan and Dr. Riyad weren't who they seemed to be. Though she tried to fight it, her knees buckled. Strong arms caught her, preventing her from hitting the floor. In a fluid, gentle motion he scooped her up and laid her on the couch, tucking a pillow behind her head.

"Amelia, are you all right?"

The sound of total concern in his voice touched her soul, but it didn't diminish the fact she'd almost fainted in front of him or that he hadn't been honest when they met. Heat simmered up her neck to pool in her cheeks as she struggled to sit. If her brothers heard about this little semi-faint, she'd never hear the end of it. In their words, she was too tough for such a *girlie thing* as fainting spells.

"Let me get you a glass of water." He quickly asked, "Where's your kitchen?"

"Through that door." She pointed then slumped onto the couch. Great, she was in trouble and the agent they sent had to be this really cute guy with red hair, caring brown eyes, and a sexy set of freckles. Just great, she huffed as she tried to soothe her overactive nerves.

Nolan returned, handed her a glass of water, and knelt at her side. Her hand shook as she drank.

"You're not a patient of Dr. Riyad's are you?" Amelia lifted a wary gaze his way.

"No," he stated with a shake of his head.

"You weren't in his office because of any 'lock picking' problem either I'll bet," she proclaimed, keeping her gaze leveled on his. "Is that how you learned about his plans to break into Fort Knox? You found information during your 'informal' visit?"

"We've been monitoring his actions." She noted the uneasy look in his eyes as he continued. "How do you feel? Should I take you to a hospital?"

Amelia shook her head. "I'm fine, just overwhelmed."

"You have a right to be." He took the glass and set it on the end table. "Can you tell me what you remember from your office visit today?"

"What do you mean by that?"

"Amel . . . Miss Morris," Nolan stumbled over her name.

"Amelia. Please call me Amelia." She reached for his hand.

Wrong move. A slow simmer of sensual heat coated her palm and sent a fiery tingle straight to her core. It took tremendous effort not to visibly shiver from the phenomenal sensation his touch gifted her. Something about him piqued her interest even more. Though she knew she should be concerned about being connected with Dr. Riyad, she momentarily refused to focus on anything other than Nolan's sexy freckles.

Was him being a treasury agent the reason she found him so attractive? No. She chewed the edge of her lower lip. She hadn't known that about him until now. It had to be the honest concern she read in his eyes and the way he kept his gaze directed on hers as he spoke.

His next statements jerked her out of her temporary daydream. Her job could be at stake. Oh no! Amelia forced her girlish fantasies to retreat and hung on his every word.

"I believe he programmed you to do a job." Nolan cleared his throat. "Amelia, Dr. Riyad and his associate planned to use you to remove an item from Fort Knox."

Amelia's jaw dropped and her eyes

widened as she stammered, "That can't be true."

Images flashed through her head as she grappled for a breath. The essence of his words struck a familiar chord and she suspected he spoke the truth. Though the whispers inside her head were unclear, she seemed to understand what the gas masked beings said. Anger rippled through her. No one did this to her. No one used her like this at the expense of the job she loved. No one!

"It is," Nolan replied. "Do you remember anything from today's session?"

Pursing her brows, she leveled her gaze on him and stated in a cool, calm tone laced with anger. "Could you hand me my purse?"

Nolan followed the direction in which she pointed and retrieved her purse. Amelia rummaged through it and pulled out a small recording device.

"This should tell us what happened today."

"You sure you want to listen to this?" he

asked, stopping her hand from reaching the play button.

"You know what's on it, don't you?"

"Yes."

"I need to know as well." She nodded then pressed play.

An hour later, she sat stunned. Nolan was right and she had the proof. Tears welled in her eyes as she met his gaze. "All I wanted was to lose weight, not my job."

He couldn't bear to see her cry. Though he knew it broke every rule in the agency's book, he took her into his arms. Deep sobs muffled against his chest as he stroked her hair. He wanted to whisper everything would be all right, but he couldn't be sure of that fact. When her superiors found out about this, it could very well mean the end to her career. He got the impression her job meant a lot to her.

For several minutes, he sat cradling her and trying to comfort her. Then it hit him; he had an idea. Nolan cupped her chin, forcing her to meet his gaze.

"I think I have an answer to this. One that might help keep your job, if you're willing to play along."

"Is it legal?" Amelia sniffed.

"Mostly." He brushed a tear from her cheek with his thumb. Deep down he hungered to taste her lips and make this all disappear if he could. But that kiss would have to wait. The timing wasn't right. When he did sample her kissable lips, he wanted it to be under different circumstances and not one derived under duress.

Something about Amelia made him think about love at first sight. Did it exist? Looking in those hot, bright-green eyes, he truly hoped it did. Nolan gathered her hands and assisted Amelia to her feet. The casual bump of her against him lit a fire within him. He had to help her in any way he could and what he had planned didn't exactly follow procedure, but he didn't care.

For the first time in years, he wanted a relationship and a love life. Being a workaholic led one down a lonely path. With Amelia in his arms, he sensed his direction had changed. Once this was over, he hoped she'd feel the same and give this newfound friendship a chance to grow and if it led to something more substantial . . . then so be it.

"I'm not sure I like the sound of that," Amelia stated, standing within millimeters of him and staring into his eyes. Heat radiated between them, warming her soul and sending a flush to her cheeks.

Never had she reacted so ardently to someone's touch. For several long seconds, she held his hands. Something about this man shot a bolt of energy through her, making her feel alive. She didn't know him, but she wanted to. The mischievous look in his eyes made her smile. Whatever he had planned, she wasn't sure she should know the particulars. Could she trust him?

When she released his hands, coldness coated her skin, making her miss his touch. Trust was a big issue. Looking into those big brown eyes, she sensed she could trust him. He had this aura about him that soothed her soul and made her like him. And her instincts about people usually proved to be right. Yet, how could she have been so wrong about the doctor? It had to be her desire to lose weight that clouded her judgment. He'd handed her an easy weight loss option, but at what cost?

"Just follow my lead and you'll be fine." He smiled, gifting her with a sexy set of dimples. "I'll need your recording as evidence."

Her recording revealed more sounds than he'd noticed earlier. A drawer opened and closed. Nolan figured they must have gotten the gas masks and a vial of the lavender powder. Gut instinct told him that powder was bad stuff. Amelia's recorder picked up Riyad's and Mina's voices when they left the room more clearly than the device he'd planted. Their conversation suggested future plans and hinted of another party's involvement. They didn't go into detail as to who that person was or their plans.

"You can have it." Amelia handed it to him. "I hope I never have to hear it again."

"I can't promise you that." Nolan's hand lingered, touching hers. "You'll probably have to appear in court and testify. This is evidence and will more than likely be played at the trial."

Nolan's cell phone rang and he excused himself to the kitchen to take the call. A few minutes later he returned.

"Riyad and Mina have been taken into custody. They weren't in this alone. It seems they had a lab set up in a house outside the city where they were producing some new drug. I've got a feeling they tested this drug on you and everyone else they hypnotized."

"Louisa," Amelia gasped.

"Would that be Louisa Langley?"

"Yes. How'd you know?"

He grinned. "Let's just say, I saw her name somewhere."

"She's my best friend."

"Then you might want to call her and have her meet us at the hospital. I've been instructed to take you there for tests."

Chapter Seven

Three days of non-stop testing and Amelia and Louisa were exhausted. Every test possible had been used to determine the effects of Dr. Riyad's drug. Nothing concrete turned up on anything. It seemed the drug was untraceable with one exception. It had a distinctive ingredient that tended to accumulate in the root of scalp hair. Samples were collected from Amelia, Louisa, and the four female bank robbers. The results were conclusive that they'd all been exposed to this drug. After the scientist downtown finished with the powder, they knew its properties and genetic uses.

"It seems the powder turned into a gas the moment air hit it," Nolan explained. "Though they haven't finished all the tests, the preliminary theories point toward some sort of mind-controlling substance."

Every day, Nolan made a point to visit Amelia in the hospital, bringing little things to cheer her. He even made a special trip to her apartment to acquire a romance novel she was reading. But when she asked for clothes, he took a female agent with him. He felt uncomfortable collecting personal items such as underwear. Since she'd blushed when she'd asked, he doubted she was comfortable with it either. When he'd returned with an overnight bag for her and Louisa, he explained, "One of our female agents acquired the items on your lists for you."

The instant relief that flooded Amelia's face told him he'd made the right decision.

"Agent O'Connell, you think this drug helped the doctor hypnotize his clients?" Louisa asked. Under Federal protection, she and Amelia shared a hospital room. They were quarantined until it had been determined neither of them was infectious.

"That's what it looks like." He sat on the

edge of Amelia's bed and absently held her hand. He'd liked Amelia's pajamas from the moment she'd first put them on, especially the parrot imprint. When he'd commented on them, her admission of always wanting a bird as a pet added to his growing list of reasons she was the perfect woman.

Louisa was a pretty, buxom brunette with a fun personality, if you liked that type. A couple of the agents on guard did. Nolan only had eyes for Amelia. Something about her drew him in every time he was around her. He liked everything about her from her infectious laugh to her brilliant intellect, to the wondrous curves of her figure. In his book, she was the total package.

"What about those women in jail for bank robbery?" Amelia asked. "Will they be released? It wasn't their fault."

"Since the money was found in a safe in the basement of Riyad's house, the women are free." Nolan smiled. "They're being treated and released, but they'll have to report for medical observation once a week for six months."

"That beats sitting in jail," Louisa quipped.

"What about us? Our jobs?" Amelia inquired. Nolan didn't miss the sadness in her tone. From earlier conversations, he knew she loved working at Fort Knox just as much as he loved taking money from the bad guys.

"You and Louisa are listed in the official report as undercover agents for the Treasury office." Nolan grinned as he gently strummed the inside of Amelia's palm with his thumb, hoping to calm her nerves. He continued, "As far as anyone knows, you were recruited for this assignment, and for security purposes, no one outside of my office knew of your involvement."

Amelia couldn't believe her ears. Nolan told a white lie for her. Tears welled in her eyes and her bottom lip quivered. "Nolan, I can't let you . . ." He cut her off with a touch of his hand to her cheek then cupped her chin in his palm.

"No matter how it happened, you were instrumental in preventing this nut job from unleashing that drug on the world. Once perfected, something so easily administered through the air could've turned entire armies against each other, or he could've cleaned out every bank in America simply by walking in, wearing a gas mask, and opening a vial." He released her chin and gently brushed a loose strand of hair from her eyes. "Be proud of what you've helped accomplish. It doesn't matter how we got there. It only matters that we succeeded."

"Thanks, Nolan," Amelia said on a heavy sigh as she captured his hand in hers.

For a split second, she thought he'd lean in and kiss her, but he didn't. The sideways glance he shot at Louisa made her remember they weren't alone. If they were, would he have kissed her? Amelia's heart skipped a beat. Every day, stuck in the hospital, she waited, anticipating Nolan's return. She yearned for each visit and hated when he left.

The doctor entered. "I'm happy to inform you ladies you're being released."

"Finally," Louisa huffed as she stood and gathered a set of street clothes. "I'll be glad to be out of pajamas for a change."

"I'll take you both home as soon as you're ready." Nolan stood and headed toward the door. "I need to make some calls. I'll be back in a few minutes."

Amelia watched him go. The man looked fine in a gray suit.

"Girl, you've got it bad."

"What?" Amelia stammered as she quickly slid out of bed and started to change.

"Don't *what* me," Louisa jested on a laugh. "The chemistry in the air between the two of you is so thick it's got its own zip code."

"That obvious, huh?" Amelia asked. "Think he noticed?"

"Honey," Louisa laid her arm across Amelia's shoulders, "there's no way he didn't. He looks at nothing else but you." Louisa hip-checked Amelia, making her laugh. "It's about time you had a hot looking fellow chasing your skirts. Wonder what your brothers will think of him?"

"Oh, Lord. Think he'll survive?" Amelia's overprotective brothers would put him through a heavy, third degree grilling.

"I'm betting he can handle himself."

A few minutes later, Nolan returned. "You ladies ready?"

"Yeah." Louisa grabbed her bag and sashayed past. "But I've got myself another ride home. I'll catch you two later."

She handed her bag to one of the agents on guard outside the door. The agent looked at Nolan, who in turn gave a nod. A broad grin crossed the agent's face as he extended his elbow to Louisa. "I'd be delighted to escort you home, Miss Langley."

Nolan held his elbow out to Amelia. "Shall we?"

She didn't hesitate. It felt good to leave the hospital. Outside in the sunlight, she breathed in the fresh air. He led her to his car. As he unlocked the door, a man came out of nowhere, slamming Nolan into the side of the car. The keys and her bag hit the ground. Amelia screamed.

The ski mask over the man's face hid his identity. He lunged at Amelia. Nolan tackled the masked man to the ground between the parked cars. The man flipped onto his back, kicking and punching at Nolan. Punch for punch, it looked as if Nolan had him. Amelia scrambled out of the way. In an amazing feat of strength, the man tossed Nolan off of him. Nolan rolled across the trunk of the car and landed on the other side.

The masked man jumped up. Amelia ran, but he caught her, grabbing her around the waist from behind. This time he held a gun in his hand. "I'm gonna kill you. You cost me a fortune."

Recognition washed over her. That voice she knew. "Terrence?"

"Doesn't matter who I am," he growled. "All that matters is you're dead."

He pressed the gun against her temple, but she'd have no part of it. No one threatened her. If her brothers had taught her anything, it was how to protect herself. In a maneuver he didn't see coming, she did a reverse head butt and at the same time removed the air from his lungs with a swift elbow to his ribs. Crumpling to his knees, Terrence dropped the gun. Before he could react, Nolan had him in handcuffs.

Louisa and her agent were on the other side of the parking lot when they heard Amelia's scream. They got there in time to see Nolan slap on the cuffs. The agent picked up Terrence's gun and tucked his own into his shoulder holster. Hospital security guards along with the other agents on duty came running to their aid. Nolan gathered Amelia in his arms. He didn't care if everyone watched as he hugged her tight.

"You okay?" he asked. The heat of his breath against her hair sent chills down her spine. He stepped out of the hug still holding onto her upper arms as he grinned. "Where'd you learn to fight like that?"

"I've got six older brothers," she replied meekly.

Nolan laughed wholeheartedly, causing her to smile. He leaned close to her ear and whispered, "Guess I'm in for a difficult time dating their sister."

Heat seeped up her neck and pooled in her cheeks. Someday she'd have to learn how to stop blushing.

She didn't get a chance to reply before he added, "I've got to take this guy downtown. I want you taken to a safe place until we can find out if there are others working with

Riyad."

He reached in his pocket, pulled out his business card, and jotted an address on the back. He handed it to the agent who was taking Louisa home. "Take her here. Make sure you're not followed and that she gets safely inside."

"Yes, sir." The agent nodded.

Nolan turned to Amelia, shoved a key in her palm as he leaned close and in a low tone so only she could hear said, "Make yourself comfortable. Turn on the TV. It's programmed to come on and play *Jeopardy*. You don't have to do a thing and you'll be safe as long as you turn on *Jeopardy*."

Before she could ask anything, Nolan jerked Terrence to his feet and shoved him in the direction of a waiting squad car. He crossed to his car, got in, and followed the squad car out of the parking lot. The beautiful woman in the rearview held his heart in her hands and she didn't even know it. When he'd seen the gun at her head, anger fueled his movements, but he hadn't reacted quickly enough. Seeing her defend herself made him want her even more.

It didn't take long to get everything out of Terrence. He'd been hired to locate the Sacred Diamond of Shabib. It hadn't been his idea to use Dr. Riyad to obtain the goods. That had been the brilliant idea of the man who hired him. A man he couldn't name. He bragged that he normally worked alone. Upon further investigation, they learned Terrence's true identity. He was the elusive cat burglar, Tyrell "The Ghost" Swanson, wanted in connection with a multitude of heists around the world.

When he came out of interrogating Terrence, Francis informed Nolan that fingerprints helped identify Dr. Riyad and Mina. They were both scientists who disappeared four years prior after having been dismissed from lucrative positions with a German pharmaceutical company. The computers confiscated from the lab contained information about their extensive research into new chemical weapons. It appeared they planned to auction the lavender powder they labeled *Mindwarp* to the highest bidder. The bank robbers had just been test subjects. It was the Sacred Diamond of Shabib they wanted.

There wasn't a mystery man who hired Terrence. Riyad had paid a Shiite militant to hire Terrence and made him think an infamous member of a Middle Eastern terrorist sect orchestrated the whole event. Lured by easy money, Terrence took the job. Riyad believed in the powers of the Sacred Diamond of Shabib. His ancestry led back to the original owner Sheik Azir Hajeem Shabib. In his mind, the diamond and its rumored powers belonged to him. He was the rightful ruler of the desert, not these crazed militant terrorist groups.

"Think if we let him loose in his homeland

with this supposed magical diamond, he'd rid the world of terrorists?" Francis joked.

"Nah," Nolan replied, shaking his head. "That's a job too big for one crazed lunatic equipped with a stone to handle. They'd just kill him before he got close."

Several hours later, he made it home. Opening the door, he found Amelia sitting on the couch playing *Jeopardy* with Pete. His heart swelled. The most beautiful set of green eyes turned his way and caused his heart to skip a beat. Yeah, he decided. His parents were right. Love at first sight existed and he was sunk.

"Hi." A smile split Amelia's face. "Why didn't you tell me I'd be outwitted by a bird?"

"Thought he might scare you off," Nolan replied, closing and locking the door behind him.

"Nah, we're buds. Right, Pete?" She pulled a treat from the drawer of the end table and tossed it to Pete. "I hope you don't mind. Pete showed me where the treats were kept."

He caught it, ate it, then squawked, "Best buds, best buds."

Nolan laughed, shaking his head. "I see he's got you trained already."

"Let's just say," she said on a husky breath as she stood, took his hat, placed it on her head, and then circled her arms around Nolan's neck, "I'm a sucker for a cute face."

"What's your take on freckles?" He wrapped his arms around her waist and tugged her close. The playful look in her eyes heated his blood. She made his hat look good. Licking his lips, he bet she'd look great with nothing on but the hat.

"Wrapped around a sexy set of dimples," she stated on an exaggerated sigh, "they're perfect."

Knowing he shouldn't, but unable to hold back, Nolan said exactly what was on his mind. "Amelia, what do you think about love at first sight?"

Amelia leveled a gaze on him that nearly melted his soul. In a sexy

tone, she said, "I'm a firm believer in love at first sight."

"I hoped you'd say that," Nolan replied on a husky breath.

Without hesitation, he captured her mouth in a passionate kiss and knew he'd found the woman of a lifetime. In the background, Pete squawked.

"I'll take romance for a thousand, Alex."

About The Author

Tara Nina creates in a variety of ranges from steamy hot to simmering sweet, which includes paranormals, contemporaries, suspense and sci-fi. She's a Southerner living in the northern wilds of New Jersey complete with grown children, four dogs, six turtles and a mountain man for a husband.

She loves to hear from readers so feel free to contact her via email tara@taranina.com

Please don't get discouraged if it takes a little while before she responds. Unfortunately, she hasn't hit the lottery yet and has to work to battle the bills of home ownership. Being a full-time writer is on her bucket list and one day, she hopes to achieve that goal.

Join her Clan MacKinnon Fan Club/Newsletter for updates on what's new and exciting in her world. http://taranina.com/join-the-clan/

Check out her website http://taranina.com

She is also available on the following media outlets:

Facebook:

https://www.facebook.com/TaraNinaAuthor

Twitter: https://twitter.com/taranina

Pinterest: https://www.pinterest.com/taranina/